Star City Publications

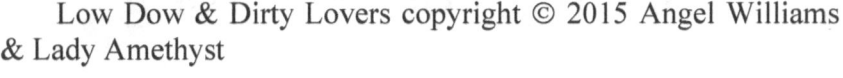

P.O Box 7322

Harrisburg, Pa 17113

www.starcitypublications.com

ISBN- 13: 9780692536667

ISBN- 10: 0692536663

First printing 2015

Printed in the United States of America

20 1 1 9 0 2 7 4 0

Angel Williams & Lady Amethyst

Low Down & Dirty Lovers
"Loving You Is Wrong"

A Novel By Angel Williams & Lady Amethyst

Things sprawl out of control when these lovers become Low Down and Dirty all in the name of love, lust and betrayal. In this dirty love triangle, deep secrets are exposed and hearts are broken. None of these lovers thought the day would come where their infidelity and backstabbing would become dangerous and possible deadly.

Acknowledgements

First and foremost, I want to give thanks, praise, and glory to the man above. Without my God, any of this would not have been possible! God has been truly blessing me, and I will always remain humble and thankful for my blessings. I have been so blessed with the amazing gift of writing, always and forever, all thanks and glory to God!

Kady Baby (Kaydence Miracle-Marie Gwynn) Once you discover your great talents. The gifts that God blesses you with you will drop Kaydence and you will formally be known as "Thee Miracle-Marie" lol yes I have high standards for you. All the late nights and the long hours of non-stop writing is for you, my precious baby. You are my motivation and my inspiration. It's because of you I push even harder and work even harder. I love you with all my heart, you are my world!

I would like to thank my mommy, Brenda Williams, who has always been here for me no matter what. She's always supporting me in any type of way shape or form that she can. My strong will comes from her. Mom, thanks for molding me to be the woman that I am. I love you.

My brothers and sisters, Joy Williams, James Williams JR., and Erica Williams thank you so much for always supporting me and reading my books and spreading the word. It's nothing like having family that always has your back!

To my lovely readers and supporting family and friends, you guys totally rock! I can't name you all, but it's some that I want to give a special thanks to who have been supporting me since day one. Without you guys, I wouldn't be Thee Author Angel Williams. ☺ I'm so grateful to have you guys as readers! Your words of encouragement are what keeps me going and going and going!!

I won't even take the time to acknowledge my haters, just know that I have too much faith in God and too many supporters for you to stop me! ☺

To anyone who is inspired by my writing and my motivation, and you are an aspiring author, just keep pushing, keep on writing. Don't stop until you are satisfied. Put hard work into what you do and love what you do. Hard work and dedication are the KEY TO SUCCESS!

To anyone who I forgot, you are always special to me and I'm grateful for having you in my life!

_____ Please put your name here.

Connect with on Facebook and Instagram Author Angel Williams (angeltherealdeal) and Twitter Star City Writer.

Acknowledgements

To my Lord and Savior Jesus Christ, I thank you above for the gift of writing. If it had not been for you none of this would be possible. I'm beyond humbled and blessed. Thanks to my loving mother Barbara Martin, who has supported, encouraged me. I love momma! I never thought I would be here, living out my dream, but faith, patience, and endurance has gotten me here. I would like to thank my deceased grandmother, Carrier Jeter for showing me what hope and hard work is. Gone but not forgotten. Marc you have been the most supportive brother a little sister could ask for. Thank you for listening and giving advice. To all my friends that believed in me since the beginning, Taneshia, Kanesha, Aletha, and Shadaria, I thank you all from the bottom of my heart. To my wonderful publisher, Angel Williams, I truly thank you for seeing what I didn't see in myself. Nothing in life is always easy, but the things that burn deep within are the things that we aim to achieve. From the bottom of my heart I THANK each and every person who played or part in this journey. Hugs & Kisses Lady Amethyst

Intro

"But I love you and you said you love me." Carmen batted her slanted eyes as she slid down on the bed.

The satin sheets hung around her waist.

Reaching her hand out she grabbed Vincent as he was trying to pull his shirt over his head.

"Please stay the night with me." Carmen begged.

Vincent stared at her and pulled away from her. "You know I can't do that. I have a wife to attend to at home. Why do you always do this Carmen? It supposed to be just fun and no fucking feelings involved, whatsoever."

Carmen held her head down as she thought about why Vincent couldn't be hers. Most importantly why couldn't he love her like he loved his wife? Yet when his wife was keeping her goodies on lock down, *she* was the one that was putting out the goods by doing anything to keep him beyond satisfied.

"Just please stay?" Carmen asked again, this time trying to push him on the bed.

He quickly pulled away from her. "Don't fucking do this shit tonight!" He had become a bit frustrated and was getting angry. *I couldn't deal with Carmen and her nagging at that moment. Better yet, at any moment at that.*

When his wife was tiring him out from all of the constant nagging, Carmen was supposed to be there to his beckoning call— doing as he says and not driving him insane.

"You know I could've stay home for all of this shit." He complained. He began moving around the room at a fast pace,

8

gathering his things together.

The ringing of his phone caused him to search under the covers for it. When his wife's name appeared on the screen, he held his hand to his lips, signaling for Carmen to hush up.

Rolling her eyes she sighed and sat back down on the bed. Staring into his mouth she mouthed the words 'Fuck you Vincent.'

He definitely reminded her why she didn't want a man; all men wore the same. Just fucking dogs and that was just that.

"I had some late work to do honey. I'll be home in a few." Vincent fussed with his wife on the other line. He got quiet as he listened to her yap on and on. "Look baby, I'm ending this call now. I'm trying to conduct business. I don't have time for the bickering right now. Call one of your girlfriends or your sister up about your girl problems." He said as he eyed Carmen. "I love you too." Vincent spoke, before disconnecting the call.

As soon as he hung up, Carmen jumped in his face and began getting on him. "How the fuck dare you, answering your personal calls in my fucking home? You tell me so much how you love me and you want to be with me, yet you keep entertaining that ghetto bitch you call your wife!"

Vincent stared back at Carmen as he slid his slacks around his waist. He was tickled inside at Carmen. When she cursed that usually was a sign of her being upset, being that she rarely cursed.

"How the fuck you like it if I tell her about us! Huh? How would you like that shit!" Carmen threatens.

Rushing over to Carmen, Vincent bumped into the edge of the bed. Carmen jumped back as she witnessed the anger growing in his eyes. She was taken back by the evil expression painted on his face. She heard so many stories about him being somewhat abusive from Keysha but she never believed it because she never saw him in action. He was always sweet and charming to her.

"What the hell did you just say to me?" Vincent asked Carmen with his hand gripping tightly around her neck.

Carmen's eyes rolled to the back of her head as she fearfully batted her eyes. She felt as if she could no longer breathe. As she was becoming breathless, his grip got tighter by the second.

"Bitch, repeat what the hell you just said." Vincent's loud voice echoed throughout the condo.

Carmen began having an ultimate fight with life and death. Of course Vincent loved Keysha, but his lust was for Carmen. She had everything a man wanted and then some more. She was drop-dead gorgeous with a nice body, well-educated and to top it off she was a very hard working woman. She didn't need a nigga or want a nigga for nothing. Well, all besides the satisfaction of her sexual needs.

Carmen realized her mistake soon after those words came from her mouth. She looked up at him in fear. "Don't you ever in your fucking life threaten me." Vincent's said in a steely voice.

"I'm sorry, but I'm tired Vincent. I'm tired of being your fucking sex slave." Tears streamed down her beautiful face.

Vincent said nothing as he loosened his death grip on her. He knew how Carmen felt but he knew that Keysha was hopelessly in love with him. He couldn't leave his wife. There was too much at stake. "Carmen, if things were different I would choose you in a heartbeat. You know how this shit goes, so stop acting like this shit is brand new. I will see you soon. I have to go home to my wife." He kissed her forehead.

She said nothing while he walked out of her bedroom as he had done so many times. Carmen felt empty and lost.

She wanted more and dammit she was going to have more if she had anything to say about it.

*****

Keysha adored her husband even when he got a little upset. She knew that he was that way out of love for her. Things with them had been rough here and there, but she tried her best. She felt like something was missing.

Keysha stared out of their bedroom window as she waited for him to come home. He worked late often. She believed that he was working something between the sheets. That was one of the things they argued about. It had gotten to the point where their sex life was nonexistent. The freaky shit that he was into, she wasn't. Carmen had told her numerous times that she needed to please her husband in all the right ways or somebody else would.

She was brought out of her thoughts when she heard the door close downstairs. She didn't really want to argue, but she knew that would come because it always did. Keysha could hear his footsteps as he made his way up.

She held herself as he entered the room. She didn't turn around and Vincent didn't bother to say anything.

He headed straight for the shower, not wanting to be bothered. Keysha sighed while sitting on the side of the bed. She ran her hands through her hair out of frustration. Keysha decided to take off her night gown and join Vincent.

Water ran down Vincent's muscular frame. He had so many thoughts roaming through his head. He was so engrossed in his thoughts that he didn't realize that Keysha had entered the shower until her soft hands roamed his back. "Keysha, what the hell are you doing? I'm not in the mood." He bent his head under the water more.

"Vincent, I just want to make you feel good." She reached around grabbing his semi-erect dick. Her small hands stroked him. As she stroked him he imaged that it was Carmen. His dick became fully erect. "You like that baby?" She asked as she stroked him back and forth. Her hand barely fit around his thick shaft.

Vincent grunted in pleasure. In a quick move he backed her into the wall and lifted her and she gasped.

"Wrap your legs around my waist." He commanded. She did as told and he entered her in one deep thrust. He fucked her to no end against the shower stall. Her nails dug into his shoulders as she cried out in pleasure.

"Shit," she moaned out. It had never been this good or intense, but Keysha wasn't complaining. It felt good.

Vincent growled roughly as he fucked her harder and faster. His mind was filled with fucking Carmen. As he imagined Carmen's tight sugary walls clamping down on him, he came with a loud grunt. "Fuck!" He held Keysha for a moment and slowly eased out of her. He placed her on her feet without saying a word. He took one look at Keysha, and that quickly he became the cold and calculated Vincent that he always had been.

Chapter 1

She stood in the mirror staring at her reflection. Joyfully she ran her fingers across her flawless chocolate skin. Her eyes stopped as she observed the scars that were underneath her breast. The thought about how closely she came to losing her life a few months back drove her crazy. She tried not to relive the past so much, but at times it happened.

She quickly shook off the horrible thoughts and focused back to what she needed to have her mind on.

The ringing of her phone startled her. "Hey, I have company. I have to call you later." Carmen quickly whispered in the phone. The sounds of her sister's desperate whimpers caught her attention.

"I can't find my husband. He fucking attacked me again and hasn't been home for three days now."

"Are you serious?" Carmen huffed. "If he attacked you, why are you even looking for him? Are you tired of this shit yet?" Carmen rolled her eyes at the thought of her sister's husband. He made her sick to her stomach. She had already informed her sister that she didn't want to hear anything about the bastard, yet her sister still confided in her from time to time.

"I just can't leave him like that. I love him. 'Til death do us a part." She cried.

"You got that right. Until he kills your ass, y'all will be a part." Carmen corrected her sister and ran her fingers through her long wavy hair. "I can't wait to tell daddy about this bastard." Carmen informed her.

"Please don't Carmen!" Her sister begged.

"Look, I gotta go. I have company. Love you." She said before hanging up the phone. She was just about to power her phone off until another call made its way through. "Why haven't I heard from you? Is your phone not working?" Carmen huffed as she got agitated listening to the caller on the other end. "Look Nik. I'm really busy, I'll see you tomorrow okay?" She said.

"But—"

Carmen quickly pressed the end button and powered her phone off. She thought about the delicious treat that laid across her California king size bed and her heart ached in the best way. The hunger for the man that she was dreadfully falling in love with as the days passed caused the quietness between her thighs to awake.

Standing, she locked her thighs a bit tighter as if it was going to help the sweetness of her juices flowing thick between her thighs. "What is this man doing to me?" Kameron questioned herself.

Her mind played an intense game with her, as she was told many times that she could play with the man her heart ached for yet she couldn't have him.

Stepping into the bedroom she shook her head as she stared at the tasteful tease that was lying freely across her bed. He was perfect in every way. He was the certified signature of epitome. He was handsome, wealthy, charming and was valid proof that chivalry wasn't dead, that it was still very well alive. Carmen felt as if God created him just for her. He had everything she wanted, even the thick chocolate utensil that pointed north as he flipped over on his back.

She licked her MAC coated lips as she thought about all the nasty things she wanted to do with him; exploring his body with her tongue.

"Kameron meet Carmen." He spoke as the beauty stepped into the bedroom.

Enviously Kameron stared Carmen down. The sway in her hips had her wondering what was resting between her thighs.

Kameron had to admit that Carmen was quite stunning. She was tall, slim but curvy. Carmen felt Kameron's eyes on her.

Spinning around she gave Kameron freedom of getting a good look at her. Kameron was much older but her body was still hot and fit, just how it was back in her youthful days. One look at her and one wouldn't have known that the milf was a spanking 46 years old. Hell she had a daughter Carmen's age.

In approval Kameron nodded. Shyly she stared at Andre who had his manhood resting in the middle of his palms, slowly stroking it until it was erect.

He felt like a king resting on his throne as he stared at the trophies— better yet queens— standing naked in front of him.

Both intrigued him having exactly what he was looking for— beauty and brains. The ability to stimulate him not just mentally but also physically. He would've died to have this sexual fixture, too bad that it was only temporary.

Strutting over to Andre Carmen's ample ass shook with the beat to her feet. Kneeling down she wasted no time wrapping her warm mouth around Andre's pole. The thickness filled her mouth as it slowly disappeared.

"Damnn." He sighed. Glancing over at Kameron he beckoned for her to come join the party.

Hesitantly she slowly walked over to the two of them. "Only because I love you, Andre." She whispered in his ear before dropping down to her knees.

Andre nodded. He knew for the love of him that both women would do just about anything that he asked them to do.

The two sex kittens fought over Andre's chocolate pole. Winning the fight with her tongue Kameron slowly flicked it over his shaft before making it disappear into her mouth, just the way Andre liked his dick to be licked. Taking up on the opportunity, Carmen wasn't ready to fight over no dick. She slowly got up and climbed on top of Andre's face, forcing his head between her inner thighs.

Andre had no choice but to lick the kitten. Kameron was highly upset. The times Andre went down on her could be counted on both her hands.

The aggressiveness in her sucking his dicked showed how upset she was. Andre's toes curled a few times as she roughly bit down on his manhood.

Sweet juices flowed down his chin and lingered into his mustache as he gripped Carmen's butt cheeks tightly. He lifted her a little above his head as he dove deeper into her wetness.

"Ohhhhh." Carmen cooed.

Reaching her hand down between her thighs, she began twirling her clitoris. Losing control she accidentally lean forward causing her to fall onto the floor.

That didn't stop Andre because he was now addicted. One taste of her sweet pussy had him craving for more. Getting up he carelessly yanked his penis out of Kameron's mouth and gave his full attention to Carmen's hot awaiting pussy.

"Fuck Andre!" She screamed out, biting her bottom lip.

Kameron set back angry with her hands folded across her chest. *This motherfucker better be glad that I don't fucking kill the both of them up in here.* Kameron thought as she enviously stared the two of them down.

Carmen began crawling across the bedroom floor and that still didn't stop Andre's tongue from connecting with her inner thighs, or stop it from caressing her hot pussy. He was really beating up her pussy with his tongue.

He then flipped her over. He couldn't wait to dig deep down into Carmen's pussy.

"Fuck baby!" He screamed out while pounding her insides with much force.

The two of them were so much into sex heaven that they had forgotten that it was supposed to be a threesome.

Kameron quickly glanced over at the duo. Angry she grabbed her things and stormed out of the room.

"Get the hell back here!" Andre called after her as he saw her rushing out the room.

Hesitantly Kameron turned around and walked towards them. She dropped her belongings. "What do you want *Andre*?" She rolled her eyes.

"Lay on your fucking bed." Andre demanded.

Kameron crawled to the top of the bed and did as she was told. Lying on her back she began to massage her juiciness with her index finger.

She crawled between her thighs with Andre's thick dick shoved inside of her. She wasted no time diving deep into Kameron's pussy.

"Ohhhhh fuck, yeahhhh!" Kameron cried out.

Carmen flicked her tongue aggressively, up and down and around in a circular motion.

Kameron massaged her breast. She never had another woman eat her so damn good. Her legs began to shake as if she were trying to do the 'Tootsie Roll'. Before she could stop it she felt the urge. "Ohhhhh! Ahhh!" She cried out as she squirted damn near a pitcher of her sweet juices all over Carmen's face.

Carmen was taken aback with all the squirting Kameron was doing. "Fuckkkk!" She screamed.

With all the excitement going on Andre began pounding deeper into Carmen's tight pussy.

"Fuck, baby I'm coming!" He cried out.

Carmen gyrated her hips and began threw her ass back and his balls pounded against her ass cheeks. Her pussy became tense. She fell to her knees. "Ohhhhh. Andre I fucking love you!" She cried out.

"Fuckkkk Carmen! Damnnnn!" Andre called as he shot hot semen all up into Carmen's tight canal.

Out of breath he fell on top of her. "Damn, girl," he said.

Kameron got up and gathered her things. She eyed Andre with an awkward smirk painted onto her face. "It was nice meeting you Carmen." She spoke before she disappeared out of the bedroom.

Carmen laid across the bed, out of breath from the harsh sex they had with her pussy still throbbing. She had to admit to herself that she was really starting to fall for Andre. Sure he was no Vincent but he definitely had captured her heart.

Chapter 2

The next morning Carmen woke up and turned over onto her side, noticing an empty spot. Her heart felt a bit empty and lonely. Things never seemed different, no matter what man she was with. She had Vincent who she loved dearly but knew he was the ultimate no no. After arising circumstances she never heard from him again. Now she had Andre who she was deeply falling for, yet she knew he wasn't fairly hers. As she thought about it, she realized that there was never a time where Andre had stayed the entire night with her; he only stayed until she fell asleep. Every time she woke up she realized that she was alone, like all other times. Was it really too much for a good woman to find a good man that truly loved her?

"Fuck love," she said to herself as she rolled out of bed and headed towards the bathroom. The constant throbbing between her thighs reminded her of the night's prior sexcapades. The smell of Andre's cologne was all over her, giving her a constant thought of him.

Just as she was about to get in the shower and take care of her morning hygiene her doorbell rung. Hesitantly gazing out of the bedroom window she noticed it was her sister Keysha.

"Ugh!" Carmen blurted. Lifting the window up she yelled to her sister, "I'll be there in just a minute!"

Keysha lifted her oversized sunglasses and gave her the thumbs up.

Carmen rushed into the bathroom and quickly released her bladder. She tied her hair up in a sloppy ponytail, threw a pair of jogging shorts and a tank top on then rushed downstairs.

Although she didn't take care of her normal morning hygiene, she still looked flawless. She deeply appreciated her natural beauty and wished a man would do the same.

"Hey." Carmen sang while she opened the door for her sister who was exactly 9 months younger than her.

"Girl!" Keysha sighed while stepping into the house.

"What's up, Key?" Carmen asked tailing behind her.

Keysha flopped down on the living room sofa and crossed her legs while folding her arms across her chest. She then uncrossed her arms and began biting her nails. She had a lot to tell her big sister but yet she didn't want her judging her and her situation. Then again she didn't have anyone else to talk to. Keysha removed her sunglasses.

"Oh my God!" Carmen sighed while covering her mouth. "Did Vincent do this to you?"

Tears strolled down Keysha cheeks as she shamefully nodded her head, admitting that her husband had beat her. This wasn't the first time that he had done so. But it was the first time that she reached out to her sister. She felt alone and deeply bruised. She couldn't let this time go without telling someone.

Carmen sat next to her baby sister and hugged her.

Keysha shyly laid her head in her lap. "I just don't know what I did wrong to him. All I'm trying to do is be a wife and love my husband." She cried.

Angrily Carmen rubbed her hands through her sister hair. They both have the similar texture of hair— dark and extra thick— except that Keysha had cut hers on her 21st birthday that she wore in a neat shoulder length bob. She had been keeping up with that hair style for the past four years.

Carmen took notice of Keysha's back and saw the bruises there. "Oh my God, Key! Did he do this to you too?" Carmen asked while shaking her head.

Keysha nodded again.

"That's it! I'm telling daddy!" Carmen said jumping up, practically knocking Keysha out of her lap.

"No! Carmen, please don't tell daddy." Keysha cried and begged. She knew if her dad had known about Vincent and him beating her, let alone cheating on her, that Vincent would've been a dead man.

Carmen ran upstairs to grab her handbag and her keys. She quickly slid a pair of sneakers on her feet. Her mind was made up. Vincent wasn't going to get away with beating on her sister. She knew from the time that he grabbed her up by her neck that he was very well abusive, but being that her sister never admitted or told anyone that Vincent was beating her, she thought she was dodging the bullet. Yet she suspected it but never got into it. Had she said something eyebrows would've been raised about the sudden curiosity and she didn't want anyone to know how dirty she was doing her sister.

When she rushed back downstairs Keysha was at the front door blocking it. Her oversized sun glasses were yet hovering over her bruises.

"Move out of the way!" Carmen yelled to her sister, while she gently tried to push her to the side.

"Please don't tell daddy, Carmen. Promise me you won't tell him. I only confided in you because I trusted you to keep this between you and I. It's bad but it's not as bad as you think it is. I went looking for Vincent and I found him drunk. He didn't mean it." Keysha began crying, covering up for her husband. As every abused and broken women did for their abuser.

"Yeah, you can tell yourself that if you want to. But I'm not believing that." Carmen spat back.

Keysha wrapped her arms around her sister, falling into her arms and crying and hollering at the top of her lungs.

The last person on earth she wanted to know that her and Vincent's love life was going down hill was her daddy. He thought so much of Vincent. He respected him as a man. He was a respectable man, with a really good job. Not just that but Vincent was able to provide for his baby girl. Vincent was a very well incredible provider and ever since Keysha and Carmen's momma passed away he never made Keysha so happy— who was the one who took their momma's death the hardest.

Carmen held her sister tightly. Although Keysha was only nine months younger than her she made a vow to her deceased mother on her death bed that she would take care of her sister and made the same promise to their daddy. After all, she was her sister's keeper.

"Okay, I won't tell him." Carmen said as she stood back, reckoning with her sister. "But I am going to have a word with Vincent right now!" She went into her downstairs closet, grabbing one of her golf clubs out of it.

"What are you going to do with that?" Keysha curiously asked.

"Don't worry, I'm not going to hurt your *man*!" Carmen hissed, walking out of her front door.

The two of them hopped into Keysha's car while she took her to Vincent's job.

Pulling up to Wigglers Law Firm, Keysha knew it was a bad idea. Yet she'd rather have Carmen approach Vincent than her telling their daddy.

Carmen had a wicked smile painted on her face when she noticed Vincent's red Porsche sitting out front. Carmen didn't give a damn if it was Vincent's daddy's law firm or not, she was ready to turn that motherfucker out and act a fool in there. Not simply for the fact that Vincent had beaten her sister, but her heart was also hurt and broken too. After she damn near got her life taken away from her by a random stranger she thought Vincent would've at least been there for her being that he was supposed to love her like he told her numerous amounts of times during and after their love making sessions. Yet he left her on her deathbed and never once did he visit her or even send her a damn card or any flowers.

Truthfully she was waiting for this day to come until she saw Vincent again. Somehow he'd been ducking and dodging her for six months now.

Killing the ignition Carmen got quiet as her mind went back to her tragic accident.

The day after she threatened Vincent, she didn't hear from him all that day. He usually would text Carmen good morning or at least a simple 'hi'. Yet he didn't text her anything.

Carmen got up in the morning and did her daily routine of showering and grooming herself. After that she headed out of the door. She treated herself to breakfast at IHOP and a shopping spree at the mall.

She was walking out of the parking lot with her oversized glasses on her face while carrying many bags in her arms when out of nowhere she heard the tires of a screeching car. Just as she was about to turn around the car came fleeing toward her and she didn't have a chance to jump out of the way. In broad daylight the car had hit her. Her and her bags went flying up in the air. Surrounding pedestrians ran to Carmen's aid as the car fled off into ongoing traffic. Sadly no one was able to get the license plate to the car. All everyone knew was that it was a black car with dark tinted windows. The windows were too dark and no one was able to see the driver. After two months in intensive

20

care Carmen found out that she was thirteen weeks pregnant and had lost the baby. She waited every day for Vincent to come by but he never did. When she would casually ask Keysha about Vincent, Keysha would say that he was working.

"What are you thinking about?" Keysha sniffled, startling the heck out of Carmen.

"Nothing. I just hate to see you going through this." Carmen mentioned, "Stay here. I'll be back in a few."

Carmen burst through the glass doors of the law firm. Ignoring the white woman's request for her to have a seat in the waiting area Carmen went back to Vincent's office.

Vincent thought he had seen a ghost when he saw Carmen's beautiful-self walking through his door.

"What the fuck you do to my sister?" Carmen yelled.

Quick on his feet, Vincent ran and closed his office door. "What the hell are you doing here?" He asked.

Carmen stood in front of the door. He couldn't help but notice how beautiful Carmen was. At the sight of her, he instantly became stiff in his pants.

"Look don't bring this shit to my work place." He said to her.

"Fuck you and your work place." Carmen snapped. She then began knocking things off his desk. She didn't stop there. The pictures of Keysha and Vincent hanging from his wall made her sick to her stomach. Tears welled up in her eyes as she knocked the pictures clear off the wall. It was obvious that Carmen was in an uproar and had come to his office for other reasons rather than regarding her sister.

Vincent grabbed Carmen and aggressively held her tightly. "Take your ass home and I will be there later!" He told her, leading her to the door.

Carmen wasn't trying to hear that. A mixture of hatred and love built up inside her. She spat in Vincent's face. Taking aback, he slapped the hell out of her. Carmen grabbed the side of her face as the tears began dropping out of her eyes. She stared Vincent in his eyes as she learned that his dark side was never too far away from him.

Vincent wrapped his strong hands around Carmen's neck. The knocking at the door was Carmen's lifesaver.

Vincent fixed his suit and got himself together and answered the door, opening it just enough to peep his head out of it. He was totally embarrassed of the mess that Carmen had made.

Carmen took the opportunity and ran past the door, bumping into Vincent's dad.

Rushing back to the car she was a mess. She opened the back door and pulled out the golf club.

Keysha looked on with big eyes as Carmen began bursting out the windows of Vincent's Porsche. That didn't stop there, she even dented up his car.

There was so much force and power behind the blows that she delivered. When she was finished her hair was standing all over her head, yet she was still gorgeous. She deeply sighed as she looked at the damage she'd done.

She was somewhat relieved. She hopped into the car and pulled off.

Chapter 3

Vincent was in a state of shock at what had just taken place. In all the months that he hadn't seen Carmen, seeing her today brought back all those lustful memories of her riding him and sucking him into oblivion. He knew now he had to see her and he was going to do so tonight. He was also going to get on his dumb ass wife for telling Carmen about what he did to her.

Keysha deserved it because at times she acted like she just didn't understand. It was hard to even believe that they were sisters. Carmen was the sexy and sultry vixen that was down for whatever. Keysha was more reserved and acted like she didn't understand shit. Vincent straightened his suit and prepared himself for his business meeting with his partners. As he sat in the meeting, comparing notes for an upcoming case, his mind drifted to Carmen.

He wondered who she had been fucking and what she had been doing. He knew Carmen all too well. Thinking of her giving *his* pussy away angered him. As soon as his meeting was over he knew that he was going to pay Carmen a visits for sure, if it was the last thing he did.
*****
Nikki was beyond pissed and she didn't like being blown off. She had been attempting to get at Carmen for a few days and she always got pushed aside. She trailed her manicured nails around the rim of her wine glass. She didn't understand what kind of hold Carmen had on her, but she feared that she was in love with her. One taste of her cream and one lick of her succulent tongue had a bitch gone.

As she sat at the bar in deep thought she heard movement behind her. She already knew who it was because they had just fucked a while ago. She knew that she was living foul because Andre was her step-father. There was no bloodline so she didn't mind doing what she did. She had to do something because as of lately Carmen has been acting strangely and distant.

Nik looked around her lavish apartment she had gotten through Andre. As long as she rode and sucked him off good, she got whatever she wanted. His wife, which was Nik's mother, was an old head, but she still looked good. The only thing was Andre was now addicted to young pussy and her mother didn't stand a chance. Andre is a well known doctor and he is very good looking. His smooth chocolate skin and physique was enough to keep your panties wet. And the rod between his legs was just oh so big and powerful. She got wet just thinking about it. At that moment she wondered if she could convince Carmen to have a threesome with her and Andre. Nik sighed wearily.

"Baby, I gotta head over to the hospital. I will get at you later." Andre kissed her neck, leaving money on the counter.

"Okay. I'll see you soon." Nik purred like a sex kitten.

Andre smiled and headed out of her apartment. She thought about her appointment with Vincent who happened to be her attorney. She got caught fighting in a public area and was charged with disorderly conduct along with assault and battery. Vincent was a good looking man too, but Nik saw evilness in his eyes and she didn't want any parts of that.

Nik got up and decided to get ready. She had things to do and people to see. She headed for the shower and did her normal hygienic routine. Once she was done showering she did her make-up and slipped on a form fitting dress. The dress hugged her curvy frame well. Her ass was sitting right and she knew that she would be rewarded quite a few male stares. Her flawless caramel skin shone and her wavy hair hung around her shoulders in loose curls. After giving herself a complete once over she headed out to see what this day would bring.

*****

Andre was sitting back in his office looking over a patient's chart. He thought about how he was sleeping with Kameron's daughter. She was only 19 but she was just so tempting. Her sultry ways reminded him so much of Carmen— a freak in the sheets and a woman in the streets, just the way he preferred his ladies. Then there was Carmen with her flawless Beauty. He stiffened in his slacks thinking about the last time he was with her. He shook his head at the memory. A knock sounded on his door and he assumed that it was either one of his colleagues or Nurse Hammerstein.

"Come in!" He yelled, ducking his head to continue reviewing what he was looking over.

"Hello Andre." Carmen's sultry voice filled the room.

Andre let his eyes slowly roam her frame as he took in her beauty. It was like she knew that he was thinking about being inside her tight, sugary walls. Carmen flipped the lock and removed her clothes, standing only in her red bottoms.

Perking her chest up in the air, she flipped her hair over her shoulders as she tastefully ran her tongue across her lips.

Coming to bring him a sweet delicious lunch was something that she had been doing for months now. She knew how sometimes dealing with unhappy patients could be frustrating and stressful, so being the good woman she was she made sure she always put him at ease.

Andre slowly stood to his full height of six feet and walked around the desk and posted up against it. Carmen walked over to him as if she were on a runway. She slid her hands up his muscular chest and pecked his lips. Andre's hands roamed her backside. No words were needed. Andre knew what time it was and he didn't even play about it.

Carmen kneeled down, undoing his expensive slacks as she looked up at him with a sexy grin.

"I hope you were taking a much needed break because I've come to give you your afternoon jump off." With those words she whipped his impressive member out and took him deep in her mouth.

Chapter 4

Kameron stepped out of her luxurious Beamer and looked up at the law firm with Wiggler engraved in gold letters. She knew that what she was doing was a deadly thing to do, but she knew, or at least she *felt*, that Andre was still fucking with Carmen. She saw how taken he was with her and during the threesome he showed her way more attention than he did his own wife. Not to mention the look they gave one another. The way their eyes locked with one another made an abundance of hatred grow inside of her. She couldn't stand these young chicks nowadays, walking around, looking fall fine and screwing any and everyone's husbands. Being that it was so many husband snatchers out there was the main reason why she made sure she maintained a smoking hot body and always kept her beauty on one hundred. Of course Kameron was 17 years older than Andre, but that didn't stop her from getting what she wanted.

She remembered when they first married and how good things were. As time passed it seemed that Andre wasn't as satisfied sexually as he once was. She would lick and suck his thick member all day and night and yet he still wasn't satisfied. She even opted out of her no's and began bringing in sex toys, even allowed him to do anal just to keep him happy. That kept him a float for awhile then he would be back to unsatisfied with their sex life yet again. So that's how Carmen came into the picture. Kameron agreed to do this only because she loved Andre and she wanted to make sure that she kept him satisfied. Needless to say, she was a real wife, she did just about *anything* to keep her husband and her family together. Here as of late it seems that Carmen had been doing all the *satisfying.*

She smoothed her hands down her expensive pantsuit and headed up to the glass doors. Returning the gesture she greeted people as they spoke to her. Kameron got appreciative stares from men and snide looks from women as she made her way to the elevator. It didn't matter where she went, she always got that attention. She just wished her husband would give her that type of attention. Sure he noticed her, but not the way that he noticed Carmen. She and Andre had met one night after a benefit and the attraction was definitely fatal. There was no way to deny it. They laughed and talked about everything. Once she revealed her age, that didn't deter Andre. In fact it intrigued him all the more.

Ever since he was yay-high he was always told that he was going to marry an older woman, being that he was always overly mature for his age. He always held a more mature conversation with older folks and not to mention how the older women used to go crazy over him. There wasn't a day that went by that he didn't shower Kameron with attention and love. Now it was a strain of sorts and she had to scare him a little.

She crossed her arms across her chest as she envisioned Andre and her relationship. She really had to find a solution to keep her man happy because there was no way she was going to lose him to Carmen or any other woman at that.

She got off the elevator and headed down the hall where she needed to be. Kameron stood in front of the receptionist's desk and looked around at the lavish law firm. It screamed nothing but money.

The receptionist looked up, gracing her with a warm smile. "How may I help you?" The receptionist asked folding her hands on top of her desk.

"Yes, I'm here to see Vincent Wiggler."

The receptionist pressed a button on her phone to buzz Vincent. She said a few words and then asked Kameron who she was. She passed the information on to Vincent and a few minutes later the cheerful receptionist was sending her down the hall.

She knocked on the door that read, *Vincent Wiggler*. This was her first time meeting him and she didn't know how this was going to go. All she really wanted to do was just put some fear in Andre's heart to make him realize what he could possibly lose. So engrossed in her thoughts she didn't realize that the office door had been opened until she stared up at a set of full lips. Vincent was gorgeous and he looked to be around her husband's age. For some odd reason she had a thing for younger men that knew how to handle themselves well like 'big boys'. Vincent was tall and had muscles where it counted and you could tell that he knew his way around a woman's body.

"Oh hello, I'm Kameron Fuller." She extended her hand to Vincent.

"Mrs. Fuller, please come on in." Vincent stepped to the side and let her enter.

She strutted into his office, looking around, and she knew that he was checking her out. She got satisfaction in knowing she had that effect on Vincent.

Vincent was already in enough deep shit, but he couldn't help but wonder what the deal was with Mrs. Fuller. She was a very beautiful woman. He knew that she was older than him, but she didn't look a day over 35. He had his wife and Carmen to deal with. He didn't think that adding another woman onto his To Do List would be such a good idea. Vincent strode behind his desk and watched her for a few moments admiring her regal beauty.

"So Mrs. Fuller, I have here in my notes that you are thinking of divorcing your husband. Are you sure that is something that you really want to do?" He studied her as she crossed her legs.

"I'm not sure, but I know at this point it's what's best. Things have changed and I know that there is someone else that holds his attention and she could possibly be holding his heart at the moment. Basically I know he is fucking someone else." She pursed her lips in deep thought.

Vincent wasn't put off by her blunt attitude. He was actually turned on. If it were Vincent he would just get even. "Do you have proof that he is?" He raised his brow in question.

Kameron sighed because she didn't have actual proof, but she knew. And she knew exactly who it was. A thought of getting validated proof crossed her mind. With an envious smile painted on her face she thought about another three some, but perhaps this time it could really go on record. In other words... on camera.

"I know that what I'm about to say is going to sound crazy, but it's what I know," she sighed heavily and looked at Vincent head on. "I don't have proof, but I know who it is because my husband and I had a threesome some time back."

"Elaborate Mrs. Fuller." Vincent flourished his hands as he sat back in his seat. He couldn't help but want to hear all the naughty and glory details.

"Please call me Kameron. You make me feel older than what I am." She smiled coyly.

Vincent took in her sultry voice and stared at her. He knew that this woman wanted him, but it was too risky and he didn't need any more drama in his life. But damn if his dick wasn't twitching behind his zipper. "Well since you know who it is do you mind elaborating?" He asked leaning forward, enough to get a great view of her plumped breast.

Kameron tucked her lips between her teeth. "Her name is Carmen Jones."

Chapter 5

Nikki had to make some pit stops before going to see Vincent. As she drove through the city her mind strayed to Carmen. She didn't know what it was about her that made her feel the way that she did. If she had to choose between Andre and Carmen, it would no doubt be Carmen. She had a powerful hold on her and she hated it. She pulled up to Carmen's high rise apartment building. Stepping out of the car she looked around like always. She looked and felt like a runway model as she strutted inside so that she could go up to Carmen's apartment.

Nikki stood outside of her door and took a deep breath before ringing the bell. She pressed the bell, scanning the halls. She knew that she was taking a chance because it could have been anybody here, but Nik didn't care at all. It had been too long and she needed to see Carmen like yesterday. The door swung open and a beautiful girl that resembled Carmen answered the door. She had some bruises on her face, but you couldn't deny how beautiful she was.

"Hey I'm Nik, is Carmen here?" she asked, looking up and down the beauties frame.

"No she isn't here, but you can come in and wait for her. I'm her sister by the way. I'm Keysha Wiggler." She smiled. The Wiggler's name rung bells around town. The promising name Keysha always made sure she announced it with nothing less than pride and great dignity.

Nik paused for a moment because she wondered if she was Vincent Wiggler's wife. She walked in and was going to keep that tad bit of info in her memory bank.

She watched Keysha as she moved around the apartment. Keysha had a body almost like Carmen's. Even though it wasn't as defined as

Carmen's it was still something nice to look at. Nik tried to shake those thoughts away from her head right away. Her main focus was Carmen. At least that's what she was trying to tell herself.

"So Nik, how do you know my sister?" Keysha stared at her, admiring her beauty.

Nik took her hands and flicked her hair behind her head. "It's a long story. All I will say is that we are *good* friends." She smiled revealing her perfect white teeth.

Keysha nodded and continued to stare at her. She looked away and Nik surprised her by lifting her chin.

"I don't know what happened, but you are too beautiful to be so down. Stop letting him abuse you." Nik said in a sincere tone.

Hearing those words made a tear escape down Keysha's cheek. She was tired of crying and feeling like she wasn't worthy of Vincent's love. Here she was and a complete stranger was telling her how worthy she was, yet her own husband couldn't realize that. Somebody was getting the love and attention that she once was and it was breaking her down. Keysha hadn't ever dreamed of cheating on Vincent until now. She had the intense urge to kiss Nik. It was something about her that made her feel differently. Key had never been with a woman before, but she was curiously looking at women before her. Even a few times she watched girl-on-girl pornos and slightly dipped her fingers into her wetness while watching the girls perform sensual sex on one another. Key nervously bit her lip as she looked at Nik. Key moved closer to her and kissed her tentatively at first.

Key was new to this, but Nik wasn't because she took full control of the kiss. This was a different thing for Key and sadly she was enjoying. She was enjoying the kiss of a woman more than her own husband's kiss whenever he did kiss her. Their tongues moved against each other as if they had been kissing for years. Wet heat pooled between Key's thighs as she moaned into the kiss.

Nik broke off the kiss and stared into her eyes. She saw lust, pain, excitement and most of all fear. Nik was young, but she was no fool to emotions and feelings. In her young years she had been through it all. From being in love and experiencing a broken heart.

Nik pushed Key back on the lush sofa and pulled down the shorts that she had on. Next she removed her thong a spread her thighs apart. Sliding two fingers inside Key's tight sugar coated wall she rotated her fingers as her thumb rubbed against her erected clitoris. Nik watched the passion on Key's beautiful face.

"Aaaaah!" She screamed out as an orgasm tore through her body.

Nik slid her fingers from her tight cocoon and placed them in her mouth, sucking her fingers clean. "You taste good," she said as she removed Key's shirt, looking at her medium sized breast.

Her nipples were rock hard and Nik took one in her mouth while she lightly pinched the other with her thumb and forefinger. Key squirmed and whimpered in pleasure. Nik kissed down to her pelvis and stared at her before placing her tongue on her wet lips. She made love to Key's pussy with her mouth. Key rotated her pelvis as Nik moved her tongue in and out of her. That blinding pressure of an orgasm was near because she gripped Nik's head while working her pelvis frantically. Seconds later she exploded all over Nik's tongued. She lapped it up, not leaving a drop behind. Nik moved back and watched Key as she sat up. She brought Nik's face towards hers and kissed her, tasting her own juices off of her lips. The scene was more than erotic.

Key pushed her back and reached under Nik's form fitting dress and removed her thong. She pushed her dress up around her waist, spreading her legs. She stared at her pretty pink lips and licked her lips. This would be the first time that she did anything like this and she hoped like hell she did everything right. She placed her head between Nik's thick thighs and placed her tongue against the wet folds of her sex.

"Damn Keysha!" Nik screamed as Key worked her tongue rapidly against her clit.

Her legs started to shake and she knew it wasn't going to be long before she came, long and hard. Her breathing escalated and just like that she let go with a long, deep moan.

As reality set in Key realized what she had done. There was no way that she could tell her sister or even let her husband know. She had gotten caught up in the moment. She raised up from in-between her thighs and looked at Nik. She too realized the heavy weight of this moment and they both had to keep it a secret. Nik kissed her lips and went to the bathroom to freshen up. Before leaving out she couldn't help but to kiss Keysha on her plush lips once more. "I wasn't here and we never met before." She winked before heading down the hallway.

She had to go see Vincent and she hoped that things worked out in her favor or else she would have to result in her sexual wiles to get what she wanted. Hell she had to admit that she learned from the best and the best was her mother, Kameron Fuller.

Low Down & Dirty Lovers

Chapter 6

Vincent was heated when Kameron left his office. He called his secretary, canceling the rest of the day's appointments. As heated as he was there was no way he was dealing with clients. He had a bigger problem. He jumped into his rental and drove a half a hour away to Carmen's house. Glancing over in his seat, he saw the gift that he had purchased for Keysha. A pity gift in hopes of getting her back home. He had to admit with her being gone for nearly a week had him in somewhat a state of misery. He missed Keysha's annoying and nagging ass.

He sighed as he was torn on who to give the gift to. At the moment his manhood was stiffening at the thought of Carmen— the way she wrapped her soft lips around his thick member and taking it all in her mouth— and had him in a sexual trance as he craved for her touch.

He was a bit more eager when he saw her car parked in the driveway. Jumping out of his car he pounded on her door harshly.

Inside Carmen sucked her teeth when she saw Vincent's car parked outside. Yet a part of her was a bit excited.

Making her way down the steps she threw her hair up in a ponytail. Before answering the door she walked into her kitchen to grab the sharpest knife in the drawer. She didn't know if Vincent was upset and was coming to her house with the fuckery or not. Whatever the case was she made sure she was well prepared rather than stuck and defenseless.

"What do you want Vincent?" Carmen asked as she opened the door just enough for her to poke her head out of it.

Vincent stared deep into her eyes. He admired her cherubic face. Standing there he then realized that his heart was for Carmen. Needless to say he was in love and couldn't help but love Carmen no matter how hard he tried to admit that he didn't or tell himself otherwise. There was a no win battle, she had him in the palm of her hands.

"Carmen just let me inside so we can talk for a few." He spoke as he tried not to let his guard down. There was no way he was going to let Carmen know that she had him.

"About what? You leaving me hanging?" Carmen asked, leaning her frame against the door.

"Yes, I can explain." Vincent began.

Carmen tooted her lips up in the duck lip position and rolled her eyes. "You know what? I don't even care to hear what the hell you got to say."

No matter how bad she wanted Vincent and how much her heart adored him she wasn't going to let her guard down. He had her once, yet he acted as if it wasn't a privilege to have her. He treated her as if she was someone on his To Do List. True they had fun and good times, most of the times were rewarding and awarding, yet the bottom line was when she needed him the most he was nowhere to be found.

Pulling the cheap card, Vincent whipped out the gift. A way to a woman's heart was gold.

Seeing the gift Carmen cracked a slight smile. "What you think, you can just buy your way back into my life?" She said to him.

"No, I wouldn't try to do that. I want to *earn* my way back into your life." He told her.

Always knowing the right things to say, Carmen bit down on her bottom lip. Giving in she closed the front door, unlatching it to allow Vincent back into her home again. Not just back into her home but back into her life. Even worse was letting him back into her heart.

Carmen couldn't wait until she undressed the two of them. She first got bare into her birthday suit then helped strip Vincent down. His thick manhood saluted as it pointed out to her. He dove head first into her. Carefully he caressed her clitoris with his hot tongue and flicked it across it at a slow pace.

Carmen widen her legs as she gave him more leverage to dive deep inside of her. Right on her oak dinner table he feasted on her goodies. "Oohhh." She moaned in ecstasy as she gripped the tablecloth.

He sucked her clit so hard her legs violently shook.

"Ohhhhh Vincent, I fucking love you," she screamed as her hot juices shot all over his face. She didn't dare suck his manhood, it was all about him pleasing her, and hell he owed it to her.

Sliding on top of his thick pole she clenched the back of his shoulders. "Oohhh." She softly moaned as she had all eight and half inches deep inside of her. Hot juices slid out of her canal as she rose and fell up and down his dick.

Vincent grabbed her thick butt cheeks as his tongue traced around her earlobe and her neck. His hands roamed all over her ass, as he was dangerously in love.

Each stroke had the two of them nearing their lustful peak. Her nails dug deep into his back as she rode him with deep and long strokes.

Throwing her head back, she closed her eyes, as she elicited soft lovely moans.

"Damn, Carmen," Vincent moaned.

Gripping her by her waist he lifted her up a tad bit. Her cheeks softly banged against his thighs while he massaged her nipples with his tongue.

"Oohhh." She cried again, this time speeding up her pace.

The soft sex went to a harsh ride for the two of them.

"Fuck!" Vincent screamed as his hot semen shot up inside of Carmen.

She laid her head on his chest as she placed soft kisses on his neck. "I love you, Vincent."

The two of them retreated to the bedroom where they had one more round. Vincent was getting dressed while Carmen was inside the bathroom showering. She came out wrapped in a towel.

Vincent gripped her up by her neck. "Bitch who the fuck is this Andre?" He snapped, damn near forgetting what he had come there for.

"Who is Keysha?" Carmen yelled snatching away from Vincent.

He took a step back then stared her down. Carmen didn't know it but she was definitely winning him over. "Leave his ass alone Carmen and this is my only warning." Vincent said and walked over to her and placed a kiss on her lips. "I love you and you know that."

Carmen stared at him as if he was crazy. He left out the house, leaving her in her own thoughts. She wondered how in the hell did he know about Andre.

Low Down & Dirty Lovers

Chapter 7

Keysha couldn't help but think about Nik. It was like she couldn't go a second without thinking about her. She was thankful that Carmen allowed her to stay at her apartment while she took time off from Vincent. She had a lot to think about. Overall she wasn't leaving her husband. She loved him and it was until death did they part. No relationship was perfect but over mending time she truly believed that her and Vincent could work things out.

She walked around the apartment and for a second she wondered how could her sister manage both a house and an apartment? She then wondered if their daddy was the one that was keeping up the bills for his favorite daughter. It didn't take a rocket scientist to realize that Carmen was the favorable of the two. Then she wondered why would Carmen have both? Unknown to her, her older sister was able to keep up with the apartment compliments to her sponsors— Vincent, Andre and Nik.

Vincent and Andre both knew where she lived but neither of them knew about the apartment. And Nik knew about the apartment but she didn't know Carmen had a house only ten miles way.

Taking her mind off Nik, Keysha grabbed her phone and called Vincent. She didn't get an answer so she called her sister. "What are you doing Carmen? I'm bored. When are you coming back to the apartment?" Keysha whined in the phone.

"I'm actually on my way now, Key. How about we go out to grab a bite to eat and then head out for a few drinks?"

Keysha nodded, agreeing as she thought about being well overdue for an outing. "Cool, I'm game." She smiled.

"Great, it's going to be a fun night. And who knows, you might find yourself a good handsome man." Carmen joked.

"Just might." Keysha laughed.

After hanging up the phone she went and got into the shower. Dressing in one of Carmen robes she walked around the luxurious apartment. She fixed herself a cup of hot tea and walked back to the bedroom. Looking in the closet she decided on something to wear. Carmen had so many clothing, shoes and designer handbags that she could open up her own boutique and start selling her stuff. Especially since most of it was practically brand new if not gently used.

"Geesh. Who's buying Carmen all of this stuff?" she wondered while looking through the stuff. She wished that she was able to have all the things Carmen had, yet Vincent was on a budget, so he claimed. He definitely brought her nice things, but unlike Carmen's men friends he didn't hand over black cards and thousands of dollars at a time for her to splurge on herself.

Being daring she decided on tossing on a pair of Carmen's brand new Red Bottoms and picked a form fitting red skirt and matching crop top.

Pulling out Carmen's accessories she decided to wear a gold necklace and a pair of diamond studs in her ears.

She wet her hair and it instantly curled up. She heavily did her make up to cover up her bruises. Topping off her look with a coat of red lipstick she stood back in the full length mirror. She couldn't help but admire her beauty.

Carmen took a double look at her sister when she came strutting out of the apartment building. She was all chuckles when she realized that Keysha was wearing the very same outfit and shoes that Vincent had bought her about eight months prior.

She straightened her face when Keysha got close to the car. "Damn you look beautiful!" she said to Keysha, who was sliding into the car.

"You think I over did it?" she shyly asked.

"Nope, you look good. And you picked the right outfit out. I think we might be hitting up the club tonight boo." Carmen laughed at herself for speaking urban slang.

Carmen and Keysha were sitting at the bar listening to the jazz band that played softy as the two of them were all giggles.

"I have a girlfriend." Carmen whispered to Keysha.

"What?" Keysha raised her eyebrow.

"You about to meet her right now." Carmen said as she stood up.

Keysha damn near choked when she saw Nik gorgeously walking over towards them.

"Hey love." Nik hugged Carmen as she looked at Key over her shoulder. Nik winked at Key before pulling away from the hug.

"What's up boo?" Carmen sized Nik up and she had to admit that she looked sexy as hell.

Carmen was so caught up in Nik that she almost forgot to introduce her sister. "Nik this is my sister, Keysha Wiggler."

Nik looked at her and extended her hand to shake Key's. When their hands connected it was like electric currents racing up their arms. Carmen was busy trying to order a drink that she was oblivious to what was happening. Nik stepped back and took seat beside Carmen at the bar. They conversed about any and everything as they vibe to the music. Key felt awkward but tried her best not show it. Keysha hated to admit it but she was jealous of the attention that her sister always got. One day she would get all the attention and she would make sure of that.

Chapter 8

The club was lit and they all were having a good time. Nik and Carmen danced with each other and Keysha stood on the sidelines sipping her drink. She swayed her hips as she watched the crowd. She mostly watched Nik and her sister. Key decided to go have a seat at the bar. She knew that her husband wasn't at home and he was probably somewhere working as usual, or so he says. Key looked over to her left and there was a fine ass guy staring at her. She had to clench her thighs, he was so fine. He smiled her way and she shyly smiled back. In a flash the mysterious stranger came her way.

"What's up beautiful?" He leaned against the bar staring at her face.

"Hey." Key said in a small voice as she looked at the tall stranger.

They stared at each other and the way that he was looking at her made her feel a little uncomfortable. She shifted in her seat as his eyes roamed her face.

"I know you probably are wondering why I'm staring at you like that, but you look like someone I know."

"Is that so?" She traced the rim of her glass.

"Yes, and I'm Andre by the way." He extended his hand to shake.

"And I'm Key." She smiled and the conversation flowed easily between the two.

Nik and Carmen were burning up the dance floor, song after song. As Nik rolled her hips against Carmen her eyes took sight of her mother's husband and her fuck buddy at the bar. She narrowed her eyes as she watched the two laugh and flirt. She remembered that her last name was Wiggler so that had to have meant that she was married to none other than Vincent Wiggler, her attorney. Carmen hadn't realized that Andre was in the building. Nik knew that if he was here that meant that her mother was at home, alone like always. Nik was far from jealous. Andre treated her well by always spoiling her, and not to mention how good the dick was that he was slanging. She wanted nothing more from him but fun and the finer things. Truthfully she looked at him as if he was her sponsor. She wasn't looking for love from him. The person that she wanted to love and wanted love from was the woman of her dreams which was Carmen.

"Nik you seem like your mind is somewhere else." Carmen questioned as she whispered in her ear.

"I'm good. Let's head over to the private lounge." Nik said. She grabbed her hand and led the way. They talked and caught up on a few things. Nik absently rubbed on Carmen's bare thigh, but Carmen's focus was now on her sister and Andre.

Carmen felt a twinge of jealousy at seeing Andre with her sister. She knew that she had her choice of Vincent, Nik and Andre, but the point of having them all to herself made her feel on top of the world. She had all three of them chasing her and sweating her. In the midst of her thoughts Nik had slid her hands in-between Carmen's thighs.

"Carmen I need to taste you. It's been too long." She leaned in, grazing her ear with her tongue.

Carmen bit on her lip and let Nik push her panties to the side. Nik eased her fingers into her wet folds. People were milling about, but that didn't matter to either of them.

"Cum for me, Carmen." She continued to work her fingers inside her tight walls.

As soon as those words left her mouth, Carmen came, long and hard. Nik removed her fingers and sucked them clean.

When Carmen opened her eyes she looked straight for the bar and surprisingly her sister and Andre were gone.

Low Down & Dirty Lovers

Chapter 9

Vincent stared at the beauty before him. He knew that this was the wrong thing to do but it was also the right thing to do. It would keep him in the loop of what went on. He would literally kill Carmen before someone else had her. She was living on her high-horse all due to him. He spent money out of the ass on her. As long as she gave it to him the way that she did, then she would always be laced with the finest of things. As he laid back on the king sized bed at the Ritz-Carlton he waited for Kameron to come in.

He knew that Keysha was out but he didn't have anything to worry about because he knew that Keysha would never step out of line. He was more than confident in that fact. The door to the hotel opened and Kameron walked in, looking like a vixen. Her hair was hung in loose curls around her shoulders. Her long legs went on for days in the high heels she had on. She looked good and he was about to fuck her good.

"Hello, Vincent." She walked closer to bed, ogling his well-defined body.

"Hello, Kameron." He smirked as she dropped the cover-up she had on.

She stood before him in nothing but black lace, which left nothing to the imagination. She had vintage pussy and he was sure that it would be worth adding fuel to his already out of control fire. As Vincent lay back on the bed in nothing but his boxer briefs, she took in the bulge before her. She had the intense urge to suck him into a blind oblivion. Vincent saw where her eyes were going and he pulled himself free. His thick cock stood straight up as he stroked himself.

She didn't waste time in dropping to her knees. She took him deep in her mouth. Vincent roughly gripped her hair forcing her down even more. "Fuck!" He yelled as she locked her jaws around his cock. Spit trickled from the corners of her mouth. "Suck that shit, Kameron." He grunted as her head bobbed.

It wasn't long before he felt his release coming. Within seconds he was letting go down her throat. He grunted roughly as he finished feeding her. She lifted her head with a satisfied smirk. Vincent looked at her with a roguish grin. He was in beast mode and he was going to fuck her like a man gone wild. He knew that's what she wanted and needed.

"Take that shit off, Kameron." He commanded as he stood, holding his cock.

She did as she was told and waited to see what he was going to do next.

"Bend over and arch your back." He said, giving her a stinging slap on her round ass.

She moaned and obliged him in what he wanted. He placed his large hands at her waist, but a light bulb came on before he entered her. He wasn't going to fuck her raw. He suited up and entered her tight heat in a rough, deep thrust.

"Shit, Vincent!" She wailed as he pounded inside of her relentlessly.

He gripped her hair and slammed balls deep inside of her. She screamed as he fucked her like a deranged maniac, but he knew that she loved it. Her legs shook and cream slid down her thighs. That didn't stop him. He kept on working her middle. "How does it feel Kameron?" He asked harshly as he went deeper.

She could only whimper. He had rendered her speechless with the power of his dick. This is what she had been missing from her husband. Her husband didn't fuck her like this, but he would fuck Carmen like it.

"Answer m." He slapped her ass.

"It feels so fucking good Vincent." She moaned.

"Fuck!" Vincent grunted as he busted.

He smirked to himself because he had her right where he wanted her. That's where he planned to keep her. He wanted her hooked on him so that her husband would wonder what the hell was going on. Little did Vincent know, soon his world was about to turn into a complete mess.

******

Keysha looked around the home that she and Andre were in. She

47

wondered how much money he had because this place was beyond laid out. Expensive paintings, sculptures and even furnishings adorned the entire house. Andre was busy at the bar making them a drink. Key nervously ran her hands up and down her thighs, looking around. Andre made his way back to her and passed Key the drink that he had made.

"So Keysha, tell me about yourself?" He reclined next her, not once taking his eyes off of her.

"There really isn't much to tell. I'm married as you can see." She lifted her hand showing off her ring.

"So am I and that makes this all the more better." He looked at her to gage her reaction.

Keysha knew that this was a dangerous and messy game, but she was tired of being in the back burner. She was going to live in the moment and let this be what it was going to be. She sipped from her drink and placed it on the table. Key boldly stood, taking Andre's drink. Straddling him she wrapped her arms around his neck. "Andre tonight I want to unwind and do shit I haven't done before. You think you can handle that?

Chapter 10

Carmen had been calling Andre's phone for the last thirty minutes. Every time she called it went straight to voicemail. She even called Key and it was the same thing. Carmen rode past his house and he wasn't there. She knew that they had to be at a hotel. There were no other spots where they could be. Carmen knew all the spots. She ran her hands through her hair as she looked out of her bedroom window. She couldn't believe that Andre was taking an interest in her sister. Granted she knew that her sister was beautiful, but she was so reserved. Carmen was used to all the attention being on her and tonight it wasn't.

She even noticed that Nik seemed to be attracted to her sister. Carmen felt like she was losing the power that she had. This was something that she wasn't used to. She had to figure out a way to remain on top. As she continued to look out of the window she saw a car pull up. It was a car that she didn't recognize. "Who in the hell is that?" She asked aloud.

Carmen didn't have long to find out before the doorbell rang. She remained rooted in the spot she was in. She finally walked towards the door. She didn't open it right away. There was a table by the door in which she kept a gun.

Carmen pulled that gun from the drawer and opened the door to find no one there. She frowned and then her eyes caught sight of an envelope at her feet. She tapped it with her foot and slowly bent to pick it up.

Looking around she closed and locked the door. She placed the gun back in the drawer. Carmen sat on her sofa and opened the envelope. She dumped the contents out and gasped in shock, surprised and most of all fear struck her. The pictures that sat before here told her the story of what she had been doing and *who* she had been doing.

Chapter 11

Carmen was a bit shaken up after the pictures were delivered to her. She pondered on who could've sent them and who was paying a private investigator to have her watched.

After her hot water was run for a bath she grabbed herself a glass of red wine. Dimming the lights, she slid in the tub and closed her eyes as the soft vocals of Keith Sweat soothed her in the background.

She didn't bother calling her men and woman around to see if they were having her followed. Of course they were going to lie. Who would admit the truth of any of that? She knew she sure as hell wouldn't. Then her mind went back to the incident with her and Vincent. "It had to be Vincent," she said aloud. Vincent was the only one that loved her and had the money to be following her around.

The next morning she woke up bright and early. After getting dressed she went to meet her dad at I Hop. She smiled when she saw walking through the restaurant. He had on a teal colored button up with a pair of black slacks on. It looked as if he didn't age a bit. He was definitely quite a sight to look at, and to top it off he was very respectful and charming.

"Hey daddy!" Carmen cheered as he got near. Sliding out of the booth she jumped up and wrapped her arms around him. She had been so busy chasing love that she had forgotten all about her and her daddy's breakfast dates. Being that she skipped two already she couldn't dare to skip another one.

Her dad wrapped his arms around her tightly. He loved both his girls with all of his heart and there was nothing in the world that he wouldn't do with them.

"How is Keysha? I've been worried about her." Mr. Fuller spoke.

Carmen took a bite of her food and then stared up at him. "She's good. You know how Keysha is." She replied, not wanting to tell her dad about how Vincent was going upside Keysha's head. Had she promised her sister that she wouldn't tell their father she bit her tongue.

"No, I mean how is she and that Vincent doing?" He cleared his throat.

"Oh they're fine." She lowered her eyes. She hated the fact that she was lying to her dad right in his face.

He nodded as he took a bite of eggs. "How are you doing?" He asked.

"I'm doing really good daddy." She stuffed her mouth with food.

Grabbing her hand he lifted it up. "I still see no ring on your finger yet." He smiled.

Shyly Carmen stared into his big brown eyes. "Not yet daddy, but soon. I'm not in a rush. These men out here aren't loyal. They ain't all good men like you."

·"You'll find you a good one soon. Because I know both of my daughters are a good loyal and honest woman like y'all momma." He spoke so highly of his oldest daughter.

Carmen instantly began to feel a sense of guilt. She wasn't the woman who her dad thought she was. Had he ever found out that she was sleeping with her sister's husband, he would be ashamed and would probably disown her. She hated that she had to sit in his face and lie, yet how was she suppose to admit to her dad that she was in love with somebody else's husband? Even worse, her baby sister's husband who she been with for years at that. The situation was just pathetic and trifling, and she couldn't help who she loved.

Carmen listened as Mr. Fuller went on and on about her settling down. Her mind wandered off to how Vincent and her started messing around. It wasn't intentional, it was something that just happened, and from there it happened more than it should have. It was as if once the two had started they weren't able to stop.

Then to make matters even worse, they weren't just committing adultery, the two of them had unexplainable, undeniable feelings for one another.

A year and a half ago, Keysha and Vincent had got into a big argument. Carmen sat in the living room while she watched the two of them go back and forth. Neither of them were giving up. Keysha was questioning Vincent about his late work hours. It was obvious that he was doing something he had no business doing. When he claimed it to be work and work only, she was just about to believe him yet again. When his mesmerizing eyes had met with hers he showcased his pearly whites. He had won her over, all until she noticed the smeared hot pink lipstick on his baby blue button up.

"What the fuck is that?" Keysha yelled as she pointed to the lipstick.

The closer she got to Vincent she noticed the smell of a woman's perfume. She was up on him like a hunting hound with how she sniffed the perfume.

Tears wailed up in her eye. "Vincent, who the fuck is the bitch?" She screamed on top of her lungs.

Vincent was caught, but he wasn't going to tell on himself. "Keysha this is from you." He said. The entire time he kept a straight face, he was good at what he did.

Keysha turned her nose up as she pondered a bit. Raising her hand she delivered a powerful smack to Vincent's face. "The nerve of you to try and lie to me. I don't wear no fucking pink lipstick!" She said with tears falling down her face.

"The shit has to be yours! I wasn't with no damn woman! You want me to cheat on you so damn bad, then I might just go out there and do it! I'm working late hours because I'm tired of coming home to your damn never-hushed-mouth, your insecurities and your verbal assault. This stuff will drive a man to cheat." He barked.

Keysha stared at him with tears in her eyes. She then turned to Carmen as she was searching for an answer. "I hate you!" Keysha hollered like a mad woman as she ran toward him.

Carmen grabbed her sister. "Please just leave," she said to Vincent. "Let her calm down a bit."

Vincent threw his hands up in the air. With the look in his eyes Carmen could tell that not only was he angry but he was a damn liar. He and Carmen both knew that Keysha wouldn't dare grace her lips with no damn hot pink lipstick. She shook her head at him. Trust no man, she thought.

He turned, grabbing his car keys and walked out of the house.

"I hate him! Why does he do this to me? What have I done wrong?" Keysha cried.

She rummaged throughout the house, tearing their shit up—

knocking pictures off the walls and doing all sorts of crazy things.

After she was done, she sat on the sofa. "I love that man so much, but I can't be his fool." She sighed.

"I understand you love him Key. I think you and him need to really talk. I'm sure he loves you too. He takes good care of you. You haven't caught him in any action, so you can't really say that he was cheating. You don't know the truth." She advised her. Realistically she couldn't blame him.

Keysha stared at her sister, lost in her thoughts. "Just go home. I want to be alone." She said sniffling.

Standing up Carmen grabbed her things. She hated seeing her sister so hurt and upset. Yet there was nothing that she could do but offer a few kind words. She didn't have a man nor have she ever had one so she couldn't speak on a situation that she never experienced. "Just be good Key. Talk to your husband when he comes back and try to keep your hands to yourself. Everything will be just fine." She told her before walking out of the front door.

Carmen was on the way back to her house. She had just gotten on the highway before her car started acting funny. The ride suddenly became bumpy. "Fuck!" She cursed, getting out the car, noticing she had a flat tire.

The first person she called was Keysha, who didn't answer the phone. After five tries she was directed to the voicemail.

Sitting in her car, she pondered who she could call. The last person she reached out to was Vincent.

He arrived twenty minutes later. Carmen watched as his muscular arms worked the jack, lifting the car. He almost had the tire off, all up until the jack completely broke and her car went crashing down onto the ground.

"Could you be any more careless?" Carmen yelled, thinking about the damage that could've been done to her car.

Vincent stared up at her with his heart touching brown eyes. "I'm doing you a favor. I don't have to do shit for you." He sighed. He then stormed off, went to his car, popped the trunk and retrieved another jack. Minutes later he had her car back up in the air again, until that jack broke too.

"What the fuck?" She screamed. "Don't you think you are putting the jack in the wrong place? Aren't you a man?"

Low Down & Dirty Lovers

"Fuck this! Call Triple A. I don't have time to be arguing with you and your ungrateful sister. As I can see the apple don't fall too far from the tree." He complained.

Throwing her hand up in the air she rolled her eyes. Walking to the passenger side of her car she went inside and grabbed her handbag and her important items before she locked the car doors. "Just take me home. I will deal with this stuff in the morning. I'll find a real man that knows how to change tires." She barked.

Vincent shook his head as he let out a few chuckles.

Sitting in the passenger seat, Carmen watched as he took his oily shirt off. Muscles tore from underneath it. She admired how fit and tidy he was. She now saw why Keysha was fussing about him being at work all damn day and night. Out of all the years she knew Vincent she overlooked him. He was definitely fine.

Before pulling the car off, Vincent reached in the back seat. He pulled out an entire bottle of Vodka. After unloosing the top, he took three long hard swigs. Then he passed the bottle to Carmen, who shrugged then took two big swigs of the Vodka, which instantly burned her throat and made her eyes water.

Pulling up to her house, she grabbed the door handle, just about to exit until her nosey ways got the best of her. "Who was she?" She asked Vincent.

He licked his lips, "She was no one." He replied. "Have a good night."

"You too." She said, getting out of the car.

As soon as she closed her front door she heard a knock.

Hesitantly Vincent got out of the car and decided to try his hand. He was sexually attracted to Carmen and had always been. Just tonight the liquor gave him enough courage to approach her for once.

Peeping out of the peephole her heart raced when she saw Vincent standing on the other side. Carmen was flushed with anxiety and excitement that was arousing over her sister's husband.

Sighing she unlocked the door and open it.

He stepped inside as he towered over her short statue.

"Did you need something?" She softly spoke.

Walking towards her he grabbed her face and slid his warm tongue into her mouth. Together their tongues perfectly matched as they playfully toyed with each other for a few seconds.

She couldn't stop the tension of heat that rose between her thighs. One thing led to another.

"Oohhh." She softly moaned. He had her bent over on the edge of her sofa as he softly slid his tongue across her wet clitoris. Her sweet juices ran down her thighs. "Oohhh, Vincent." She cooed.

His tongue massaging her clitoris felt so damn good that she didn't have time to feel guilty about anything.

Keysha who? All she knew at that moment was that Vincent belonged to one person. And that one
person was her.

"I'm coming." Carmen hummed and her legs slightly shook.

Not stopping, his thirst was at an all time high, savoring every drop of her sweet juices. He stood up with her wetness around his mouth. Her breathing became labored as she slid her finger between her thighs and then slowly rubbed her free hand across her breast.

She turned over in time just to see his thick manhood in the palm of his hands. All over again she became hot and wet thinking about how good it would feel for his thick dick to be inside of her, penetrating her insides.

"Fuck me Vincent!" She wailed. His hard dick was nested between her thighs.

He lifted her off the couch with his dick inside of her and carried her across the room. Pinning her up against the wall he nibbled her nipples. Juices ran down her thighs. He slowly gave her long pumps.

Sliding his thickness in and out of her puddle, he effortlessly held her against the wall. She held on for her dear life while her wet pussy perfectly gripped around his thickness. The only sounds that could be heard were the soft moans that escaped their lips, the wet kisses that the two of them shared and her wetness— the sound of him sliding in and out of her. The soft strokes soon turned into long and hard.

She held on and enjoyed the sexual ride of her life as he fucked her.

"So are you fine with that?" Mr. Fuller spoke.

She quickly turned to him. She was so lost taking a walk down memory lane that she was absent from the conversation that they were having. Mr. Fuller was so busy stuffing his face, talking and thinking about his new lover all at the same time that it wasn't even recognizable to him that his daughter had dazed off into her own little world minutes prior to him babbling off.

"Fine with me having a lady friend? She's a tad bit younger than I am. Yet she's so smart and beautiful. I feel like I'm on top of the world with her." He spoke with a wide smile painted across his face.

Carmen loved to see her dad happy. He hasn't had a woman since their mom had passed. Although she was deceased, he was still loyal to her. Reaching out, she grabbed his hand. "Daddy, I hope she makes you happy. It's time for you to move on. Enjoy your life because you only have one and you're a good man, so you deserve a good woman. If you like her, then I love her." She told him.

"Thank you sweetheart. You and Keysha will meet her sooner or later." He assured her.

She nodded and went back to digging into her food.

Chapter 12

Kameron was pissed at the fact that Andre started to act very odd with her. He hadn't slept with her in days.

The two of them never had a problem with their sex lives. Sure they liked a little fun and that was about it. Besides that they were just fine. She would go far and beyond to make sure her man was happy and well pleased. There were no limitations in the bedroom when it came to her. She aimed to please; rather it was sloppy sex, deep throating, throat fucking, anal, threesomes, and hell orgies. Whatever it took, she simply aimed to please.

"Who is it, Andre?" Kameron fussed as Andre slid out of their king sized bed. It had been the third night in a row since the two of them been intimate and she wasn't too happy about that. Sure she was going around town. She had two official side pieces, yet she wanted to be pleased by her husband and didn't want him laying the pipe elsewhere.

Andre shook his head. Although he loved Kameron to pieces she just didn't sexually stimulate him lately. He slid out of bed and went into the bathroom.

Tuning all of her bickering out, he turned the shower on and eased into the luke warm water.

Kameron took that time to go through his phone. She strolled to his phone and began reading all of text messages.

Seeing a text from an unlisted number which he texted very often she took the number down mentally. She was no fool.

She didn't even bother getting in the shower. She threw on a pair of jeans and a tank top and slid into her off white thong sandals and left the house.

The first place she went was past Carmen's house, who she noticed

58

wasn't home.

She then drove to the local mall to get herself a pedicure. With all the tension that was built up, she needed to relieve it somehow and since her man wasn't giving her what she needed she decided to treat herself to a relaxing pedicure.

When she saw Carmen walking out of the IHOP across the street she had a change of plans.

"Hey Carmen. Can I talk to you for a second?" Kameron asked as she approached her.

Carmen squinted her eyes and then she remembered where she knew Kameron from. She wasn't really attracted to Kameron, she was way too old for her taste. The only reason she allowed Kameron into her home and into her bedroom was because Andre begged her to allow it to happen. Carmen was hoping that Kameron wasn't back for seconds, especially since she walked out on them during their threesome. She was not her type— old and too damn boring.

"What's up?" Carmen asked, sticking her phone back into her handbag.

She pulled out her oversized Chanel shades and slid them onto her face.

Kameron stood their enviously staring at her; she hated the way Carmen appeared to be so damn perfect with no flaws or cares in the world.

Kameron didn't bite her tongue she went straight to the punch. She was so damn upset just by looking at Carmen she dared her to lie to her. If she had, she would have most likely slap the taste out of her mouth. She hated to be lied to right in her face.

"Ummm, you know Andre, that's my husband." Kameron said holding her ring finger out, displaying the oversized dipped in diamond ring that Andre brought her.

Underneath Carmen's sunglasses she rolled her eyes. She hated the fact that Andre had lied to her. She knew he had a motive of bringing Kameron into her bedroom. Yet Kameron agreed with it. She didn't know what type of sick stuff they were into. Whatever it was, she didn't want any involvement.

Carmen decided to taunt her a bit. "I don't know what you are talking about. You need to be having this conversation with Andre and not me." Carmen said as she began to walk off.

Kameron quickly grabbed her by her arm. Taken back Carmen snatched her hand. If Kameron was looking for trouble then she sure as hell found the right place to get it.

Carmen stared at her, "Yes I am sleeping with him. He's at my house damn near every night. His head stay between these thighs. Now I won't further discuss any of this with you. Take this up with your *husband*!" Carmen snapped as she stormed off.

Kameron stood there for a second as she was lost in her own thoughts. She was a bit raged and angry the way Carmen, who was nothing more than a child to her, tried to talk to her as if she was no one.

She quickly tailed behind Carmen who was getting into her car.

Things had spiraled out of control in the quickness.

Angry, Kameron decided she was going to teach Carmen a lesson.

She roughly yoked Carmen up by her hair. "Bitch who the fuck you think I am! Don't ever get me fucked up!"

Kameron barked. Forcefully turning Carmen around she sent two slaps across her face.

Carmen quickly broke away from her grip. She was more so of a lover than fighter, but always being the pretty girl back in her high school years she had no choice but to learn how to fight. She had to protect herself someway. She drew her fist up and went haywire on Kameron. She was so damn quick with her hands, sending punch after punch to Kameron's face and body. Kameron couldn't get one hit in.

"You want trouble, here it goes." Carmen said as she snatched Kameron up by her hair. One last hit to the face,

Kameron was out on the ground, trying to force her aching body to the curb before she got hit by a car. From her falling to the ground so hard and hitting her head, blood gushed from somewhere. She couldn't find the spot, she just saw the blood and felt the pain. Kameron couldn't believe the ass whipping that Carmen had just put on her. She felt embarrassed as she forced herself off of the
 ground. Hurt and fed up with Andre's mess, tears rolled down her face as she shamelessly limped her way back to her vehicle. When she was almost at her vehicle, an unfamiliar feeling came over her body, everything became blurry and before she knew it she passed out in the middle of the street.

With a handful of Kameron's hair, Carmen stared at the people that were standing nearby watching. "What the fuck are y'all looking at?" She yelled.

She jumped into her car and pulled off into traffic.

"Andre you have a *wife* now!" Carmen yelled over the phone.

She didn't give him a chance to answer her question, "How dare you bring that bitch up into my home and have me have a threesome with her. You and her both are sick and I'm not down with that shit. Leave me the hell alone before I turn your life upside down." She yelled before hanging up the phone.

Carmen pulled up to her house and rushed inside her house.

She let out a loud piercing scream before throwing herself onto her bed. Burying her head into her pillow, she began wailing and weeping like a spoiled newborn. She was beyond hurt and frustrated for allowing herself to fall for Andre. Here he was all this time unhappily married and never mentioned the union.

Her soul ached and even worse her heart pained. She was tired of falling for all the no good men, all she really wanted was what everyone in the world wanted. To love and to be loved, yet everyone who she loved it was wrong to love them…

Chapter 13

"Dr. Fuller we have a forty-six year old whose blood pressure is rapidly dropping. It's apparent that she is losing blood from somewhere." A young nurse said.

When Andre stepped closer to the patient's bed he froze when he saw his wife laying there barely recognizable. He was at a loss and he almost lost focus. "Okay we need to get a CT scan set up and we need to continue to monitor her heart rate and blood pressure." He opened her eyelids to see that her pupils had dilated.

He had a feeling of who did this, but he just couldn't figure out how it happened and he was absent at the mind as to how Carmen had found out he was married. It was some crazy shit going on and it was causing problems on every hand. Andre and his staff rapidly worked on Kameron so that they could place her in ICU. He had to call Nikki and let her know that her mother was in critical condition. The things that happen when you are living foul.

*****

Nikki was busy doing what she loved to do best besides sex, she was busy spending money. As she walked around the Louie Vuitton store she caught sight of a very good looking man. He stood about six feet. Smooth chocolate skin and mesmerizing eyes. Nikki quickly looked away because she already had enough on her plate as is. She was dealing with Keysha, Carmen and her mother's husband. She didn't need any more drama in her life. She continued to browse and next thing she knew she was standing right in front of the gorgeous stranger. She looked up and mentally gasped looking into his face. He flashed a white smile and her stomach did flips. She looked away and in a bold move he lifted her chin making her look back at him.

"I don't mean to be all up in your personal space, but you are beautiful." The mysterious guy said.

"Thanks." Nikki said as she stared at him.

"Can I get your name?"

"Nikki. And you are?"

"Just call me Vic." He flashed another smile.

His tall frame stood overseeing hers. Staring down at her he felt powerful. One thing he loved was a gorgeous woman.

Nikki stared at him as he grabbed her hand, kissing the back of it. It was so mysterious and he sent chills down her spine. It was something about him that she couldn't put her finger on. Vic gave her the impression that he was a dangerous pretty boy that didn't follow rules but broke all of them.

"Okay Vic it is." Nikki flashed a smile feeling like she was getting connected with the devil himself.

He was just about to say something else, but her phone rung breaking the magic moment. She fished her phone from her handbag and saw Lancaster Memorial calling. She frowned and turned answering the phone.

"Hello."

"Nikki you need to get down here fast. There has been an accident; your mother was severely beaten." Andre said in a rushed tone.

"Oh my God, I'm on my way." She hung up and pushed past Vic.

"Hold on." Vic grabbed her arm lightly.

"Look I have to get to the hospital." She pleaded.

"Here take my business card and call me when you get some free time."

She nodded and looked at the card quickly leaving out the store. Nikki had no idea that Vic was Vincent's younger brother and he was there to stir up much trouble. He knew all about the low down and dirty shit that everybody had going on; especially his brother.

Angel Williams & Lady Amethyst

Chapter 14

Carmen had been on lock down for the last few days. She hadn't talked to Keysha and she sure as hell hadn't said anything more to Andre. It was odd that she hadn't talked to Nik because she was constantly blowing up her phone.

Today she was hid out in her home instead of her apartment. Since she knew somebody was watching her she decided that it was time to chill out for a little while. She thought back to the other day when she had breakfast with her father and remembered that he was dating someone. She was curious as to who he could have been dating. She just hoped that he didn't get caught up in any drama like she had. That made her think about Keysha and what could have possibly happened between her and Andre. She didn't think Keysha was that stupid, but then again you just never knew. She flopped back on her bed looking up at the ceiling.

Her doorbell sounded and she got up, thinking she knew who that was.

She stood and walked towards the door. Without looking out she opened the door and stared into Vincent's face. She blew out an exasperated breath and let him in. "What the hell do you want, Vincent?" She took a seat on her sofa.

"I think that Keysha is cheating on me." He looked distraught.

Carmen laughed knowing it was going to piss him off, but this was hilarious. He comes here knowing he fucks me every way he can and now he wants to be hurt because he feels like he has been done wrong.

"Well you are doing the same damn thing Vincent."

"That's different. She knows that she belongs to me and only me. You supposed to belong to me too, but you too busy fucking and

65

sucking other niggas." Vincent glared at her. "All y'all hoes are just the same," he had the nerve to say.

"But I'm not married though so I can fuck and suck whoever I want to and whenever I want to!" Carmen smirked.

"Bitch don't you ever talk to me like that." He back handed her causing her head to snap back.

She held her face not believing that he hit her. She was starting to see the Vincent that her sister saw often and she didn't like it all. She looked up at Vincent and she saw rage in his eyes. In that moment she feared her life.

"Baby I'm sorry." He reached for her, but she moved away.

Vincent picked her up and took her down the hall to the bedroom. He was just in his feelings because he couldn't handle the fact of Keysha possibly cheating. It was okay for him to do so, but not her. It was a double standard he knew, but it was just the way things were.

"Carmen, baby I'm sorry." He kissed all over her face.

Tears streamed down her face as he kissed her. It was bad enough that all the drama in her life was having her in a ray of anger, then here was Vincent bringing more shit to her house.

Even through his rage she knew that he loved her and sadly she loved him, but what they were doing was soon going to end or else someone was going to end up hurt. Both of them were confused and deranged. Vincent lay down next to Carmen, planting kisses all over her body. He held her body close to his and closed his eyes until the two of them drifted off to sleep.

Low Down & Dirty Lovers

Chapter 15

Nikki had gotten to the hospital and she rushed through the ER. Frantically she rushed over to the front desk. As soon as she hit the front desk, Andre appeared. He engulfed her tightly and she took comfort in his arms.

"What happened?" She pulled back looking into his face.

"Nikki, I really don't know what the hell happened." He said knowing, but couldn't tell her what he had been doing. Hell he was doing her too. He knew soon or later, a lot was going to be happening and honestly he wanted no parts of the repercussions.

"Why do I get the feeling that there is more to this whole story than you are letting on?" She folded her arms.

Andre didn't say anything he looked at the nurses moving about as he leaned one arm on the counter. Things spun out of control when Nikki came to live with them after things didn't work out with her father. When he first laid eyes on her, he knew that he had to have her. She was young, sexy and was a freak. He knew that sneaking into her room at night was a deadly game, but he loved feeling her tight, sugary walls wrapped around his shaft. Not only that he had to get involved with Carmen then her sister which he felt a strong connection to.

"There is, but right now let's go see your mother." He ushered towards the elevator so that they could to ICU.

As the elevators door opened Nikki looked up and saw Vic. He grinned and flashed a wink as he got off. Andre saw the exchange and frowned. "Nik who the hell is he?" Andre glared at her.

"Uh someone I met earlier." She shrugged nonchalantly.

Andre stared down at her not saying anything. He didn't like the fact that she was possibly doing her thing. He was the one who popped her cherry. She was pure when he had her and wanted it that way, selfishly he had no plans on having any sort of relationship with her. He just wanted her only touched by him until he got done playing with her, which Nik already knew. Andre expressed on many occasions that her and her pussy belonged to him and him only. He told her numerous of times, no boyfriends, yet he failed to mention that she wasn't allowed to have any girlfriends.

Sadly Nik had been doing her thing with Carmen and Keysha and he didn't have a clue.

Chapter 16

Vic was making his presence known and he was so slick about it. His brother had no idea that he was back in town and he planned on keeping it that way. Before he had left town it was a few months before Keysha and Vincent had actually tired the knot. Vincent and Vic were sharing an apartment located in Uptown New Jersey. One night after having a few beers, things between the two of them sprawled out of control. First it was an innocent talk about their mother who committed suicide a few years back. The outcome of that was both of her sons were heart broken. Vic, the youngest, took her death the hardest. Since then he had been a functional drug addict and an evil alcoholic. The innocent conversation about the mother soon turned into an argument.

"You are the reason why momma killed herself." She was tired of always doing everything in her power to please you. Not to mention all the stressed your unstable ass had put on her." Vincent shouted to his younger brother. Angry Vic jumped on Vincent and the tussling began until they were throwing punches at one another, trying to knock each other's head off.

After that fight, in the middle of a snow storm, Vincent put Vic out on the streets with nowhere to go. Vic didn't even fight back, he left, leaving New Jersey all together. He vowed that when he came back to town, his cold hearted brother was going to feel his wrath my any means.

Nobody knew that Kameron had hired Vic to get dirt on Vincent. Vic took it to another level by going deeper and digging deeper. He knew who was sleeping with whom including who Kameron was too. She wasn't in the clear either. As he got outside to his car he thought about what his next plan of action was going to be. First he had to get him something to eat. As he hopped in his Mercedes he decided to go around the corner to the corner café. He parked and got out and went inside. He took a moment to look around and he caught sight of his brother's wife, Keysha Wiggler.

She was beautiful and he couldn't understand why the hell Vincent treated her the way that he did. He walked up and ordered his food. As he waited he continued to stare at her as she looked out the window. He had already made up in his mind to go sit with her and see if he could get in her head a little bit. Once his order was ready he strode over to her and took a seat. Her beautiful eyes took him in and she turned away.

"Why are you sitting her looking like you lost your best friend?" He took a sip of his drink.

"Maybe I did. Why you here and who are the hell are you."

"Hopefully I can be the one that puts a smile back on your beautiful face." He winked causing her to blush. Had his brother not put him out many years ago, she would have met Vic.

Keysha could only stare and wonder what was up with him. It was something about him that she couldn't quite put her fingers on. As she studied him he reminded her of someone hell in a way he favored Vincent. Maybe she was just imagining things.

****

Vincent left Carmen's house as she slept. He was supposed to meet Kameron a few hours ago and surprisingly she hadn't called. That was really odd. He drove through traffic thinking about the mess that he had created. It was too late for regrets because he was already in too deep, especially with Carmen. He felt that danger was near because his muscles became taut and he was on edge. There was so much secrecy going on and he was the ring leader of it all. He was just glad that his wife hadn't gotten caught up in all the nonsense that was taking place. He tried calling Carmen for the fifth time and there was still no answer. Something was terribly wrong and he knew it. He was going to let it go for now. Vincent decided to go home and spend some time with his wife. Maybe that's what would be best for him now. He turned into his driveway and realized that Key's car wasn't there. He sat there trying to figure out where she could be. He quickly grabbed his phone dialing his wife's number. The phone rang and rang with no answer. "Where the fuck is she?" He yelled hitting the steering wheel.

He decided to call Carmen to see if she had talked to her. Once he confirmed that Carmen hadn't he became worried or better yet angry. She knew better than to ignore any of his calls. Vincent wasn't used to this because he was so used to her always blowing his phone up nagging about something. He called Keysha one more time and finally gave up. Vincent got out of his car and decided to just go inside before he ended up doing something stupid. He decided to take a shower. As he stood under the water his thoughts strayed everywhere. He couldn't believe how far he allowed things to spin out of control, but it was just such an enjoyable ride. He finished his shower and wrapped a towel around his waist. He walked into his kitchen grabbing a beer. He twisted the cap and took a much needed drink. There was a knock on his door and he went to answer to find Nikki on there. She looked like hell and he hadn't seen her since he helped her a while back.

"Nikki, what are you doing here?" He asked.

Nikki couldn't focus because she stared at Vincent's amazing body. She let her eyes roam below the towel and there was bulge there. She licked her lips and all rational thoughts left her brain. She knew that this was crossing the lines, but right now she just needed to be loved if only for a little while. Keysha or Carmen were not available and he was the first person that she thought of.

"Vincent I didn't know where else to go. My mother is in the hospital from being severely beaten. Her husband isn't saying anything, but I feel like it's more to the story than what he is saying." She looked up at him with tears in her eyes.

"Come in." He stepped aside and let her in.

She stood there looking around. Vincent came up behind her and ushered her to the sofa. They sat in silence for a few minutes before she spoke again. "Vincent I get the feeling my mother has gotten caught up in something, but I'm not sure what. Somebody attacked her, but I don't know why or what for." She sighed as a lone tear slid down her cheek.

Vincent didn't say anything right away as he took in what she was saying. It seemed like drama was surfacing everywhere.

"Who is your mother?"

"Her name is Kameron Fuller."

******

Andre kept calling Carmen's phone, but there was no answer. He knew that she was probably looking at the phone, ignoring him. He was going to pay her a visit. He knew that she was probably hiding away at her house today and there was no need for hiding. He was five minutes away from her house and he had to get down to what the hell was going on. Seconds later he pulled up at her house. He got out banging on the door. "CARMEN OPEN THE FUCKING DOOR!" He yelled.

The door swung open and he was about to light into her ass until he saw that her face was bruised and swollen. He went to touch her face but she flinched as she moved back. She felt so low and now she understood how her sister felt. She wanted her sister man and that she got, along with the abusing that he came with. She learned the lesson first hand, that everything that looked good sure as hell wasn't good. What was good for one person, wasn't always good for the next.

"Carmen, what happened to your face and who did this to you?" He stepped into the house closing the door.

"It doesn't matter. I brought this on myself. What the hell are you doing here? Shouldn't you be with your wife?" She rolled her eyes.

"Carmen my wife is the reason that I'm here. She is in ICU.

Chapter 17

Carmen stared into Andre's eyes. And for once in her life she decided to tell him the dirty truth. Well at least part of the dirty truth.

"Look Andre it's a lot going on in my life right now. I'm not the person who you think I am. I understand we may have feelings for one another, but this isn't going to work. When you brought Kameron into my home, you never once told me that she was your wife. The times you made love to me, you never once told me you were married, which is now fine when I look at the bigger picture. I haven't been just sleeping with you. I've been sleeping with another woman and even worse another's woman husband and you. And for the record, I didn't attack your wife first, she attacked me, in defense I did what I had to do to protect myself. And I'm not sorry for what I did. But I am sorry for falling for you, it's time that we end this today." She spoke.

Andre stared at her shaking his head, it made sense that Kameron very well had went looking for trouble, writing a check that her ass couldn't cash. Inside Andre was actually laughing at the fact that Kameron got herself beaten up.

It wasn't good walking around pretending to be Mrs. Billy Bad Ass.

Andre sat and thought for a second about what he had with Carmen and then his relationship with his wife and Nik. When he was with Carmen he felt like a totally different person. He actually felt like he was being loved by the way she catered to him. When he was with Kameron he felt loved as well, yet he felt like the love was a bit different. He felt more so that she was more of a mother figure that he was always searching for more than anything. When he was younger, he was thrown into a foster home. Later in his life he found out that his birth mom had passed away a few years back and his dad was left unknown. He never had the mother and son relationship, so when he got with Kameron he felt some sense of security that he was looking for. She took good care of him, sexually and physically. She pleased him and helped with everything and anything he needed.

Andre's mind was made up, he was a respectable man and had good credibility, and he needed a woman that could hold his interest. No matter what Carmen told him she had done, to him it was all in his past. He needed love and to be loved, already he had forgave her... Plus his past wasn't so squeaky clean either.

"Carmen, I'm in love with you. Let's leave this place and start all over." He said grabbing her hand.

Carmen looked at him, she badly wanted to take him up on his offer then she remembered the saying, what comes around goes around.

"Andre, this is something I have to think about. I just can't get up and leave. And how can I trust you. I'm afraid you'll do the same thing you did Kameron to me. Who's to say when you get bored with me you will go find the next female to keep you happy?"

Andre thought for a second, Carmen was making a great point, but he could care less. At that moment he wanted to be with her and strictly with her. It would have taken a lot of adjusting to do but he could be faithful and loyal to just her and her only.

"Look this is my first time ever stepping out of my marriage." He lied.

Carmen looked in his eyes and wanted to believe him, knowing better she knew him as nothing more than a liar. Once a liar, always a liar to her. "Let me sleep on this." She stated while standing up. She stood to her feet and looked towards the door.

"Are you expecting company?" Andre enviously questioned.

Carmen smiled, "No, I just want to be left alone for the time being." She explained.

Andre was a bit sad that he had come all the way to Carmen house and didn't conquer anything. But hey sometimes it be like that.

Chapter 18

After Andre left Carmen's house, he went to the next person on his list which was Keysha. He knew that things between him and his wife were never going to be the same again, which he didn't give two shits about.

Indeed he loved her, he was just no longer in love with her and it had been like that for quite some time. They had discussed the issue on numerous occasions and that was the start of them allowing other women into their sex lives. He was thankful all that Kameron had tried to hold on to their relationship. It just wasn't working any longer and he refused to try to mend something that wasn't there. At the end of the day, he wanted to be happy not miserable for the rest of his life because he was so busy trying to make someone else happy. On top of that, he knew Kameron was seeing someone else. On many occasions she had come home past respectable hours and was lingering with the scent of Guilty Gucci, a cologne that he had retired from for months now. So that was valid evidence that there was in fact another man in her life.

"I'm not happy and you're not happy." Andre expressed to Keysha who had just creep out the house and met him down the street.

Keysha leaned over and placed a few small pecks on his lips, intentionally the pecks turned into a battle between their tongues. Sliding his hand between her thighs, he felt her puddle was sticky and slippery. He eased his fingers in and out of her.

"Oohhh, Andre." Keysha softly moaned as he fingered her in the front seat of his Beamer truck.

Keysha broke loose from their kiss and slung her head back. Slowly she gravitated her hips in a circular motion as she thrust her midsection against his finger.

Andre seductively pulled his fingers out of her stickiness, licking all of the sweet juices off of his fingers. He then shoved his fingers into Keysha's warm mouth. Savoring the taste she seductively licked the left overs off of his fingers.

The two of them never once took notice of the all black Lincoln Town car that sat across the street from them.

The driver snapped picture after picture.

Vic had to admit Keysha was definitely sexy, he wouldn't have mind having a peace of her. Catching her in full throttle action, he still felt bad for her. In his eyes she had every reason to what she was doing. Her husband was a no good dirty bastard and had been doing her dirty for years.

Getting enough footage for the time being, he placed his camera in the back seat. He was pretty sure to have more footage later being that the no good, low down and dirty lovers couldn't keep their legs closed.

He watched as Andre raised Keysha shirt, showcasing her perky mouthful breast. Her erect nipples stood salute as he became sucking on them.

"Fuck!" Vic cursed to himself. He couldn't believe how aroused he was becoming from looking at the two put on a sex show in front of him. The scene was worthwhile. Being the freak he was, he unzipped his pants and saluted was a thick nine-inch pole.

Watching the two he stroked himself up and down, in a matter of seconds. He was catching hot semen with an old shirt that he quickly grabbed from the back seat. He licked his lips. He was definitely going to soon have a taste of Keysha, if that was the last thing he did. He came back for revenge and he'd be damned, revenge was definitely what he was going to get.

Before leaving the scene he felt awful for what he was about to do, yet it had to be done.

He pulled out his cell and dialed the familiar number. Before he could even so anything over the phone, he noticed Vincent's car pulling down the street.

He quickly honked his horn and a startled Vincent looked to his left and noticed his wife ducking down in the front seat of someone's car.

Angry Vincent jumped out of his car, "What the fuck is this?" He asked snatching Andre's door open.

Andre was caught off guard and before he could do anything

Vincent sent three quick jabs to his face.

"No, he's just a friend. It's not what you think it is Vincent." Keysha screamed trying to spare Andre's life.

Vincent gave her the evil eye as if she was crazy, Keysha squeezed her thighs together as fresh juices were still running down her thighs.

She rushed over to Vincent, jumping on his back like a maniac she started pounding on his head.

One sling and she went crashing to the ground. Vincent pulled Andre out of the car, Andre stood up on wobbling feet. Vincent sent another punch to his face, a kick to his stomach, blood splattered everywhere.

"Ahhh." Andre cried out in agony.

He fell to the ground. Vincent ran up on him and stomped him dead in the middle of his back. Andre could feel at least two of his bones cracking.

"Who the fuck you think you dealing with, coming around here fucking with my wife!" Vincent roared like the mad man he was. Keysha stood back, tears ran down her face she was so afraid for Andre's life and worse her own life she feared was soon going to be taken.

Vic rolled his window down and snapped some good shots of the fight. It was funny how things was just falling so much into place without him doing a thing.

Sirens were heard in the background. Ten minutes later, Keysha was hopping in the back on the ambulance with Andre and Vincent was being placed a handcuffs as his Miranda rights were being read to him.

Vic pulled off, "Karma is a pure bitch who has no sympathy for no one." He said to himself while cruising down the street.

Chapter 19

Kameron had been released from the hospital. She was furious, humiliated and the devilishness she was possessed with she wanted nothing more than sweet revenge. When it came to Carmen she had pure hatred in her heart, she wanted her dead, wiped clear off earth by any means. She tapped her foot as she waited outside the hospital for Andre. He still didn't make it there yet. He told her he would be an hour and it had been way past an hour. She tried calling Nik who wasn't answering the phone either.

She was just about to call her sugar daddy that she was really falling in love with by the second until her phone beeped indicating that there was a message. The constant beeping indicated that there was more than one message being sent to her. Curiosity was raised to the highest level as she hurriedly strolled through her phone to the text messages.

Seeing the picture messages she was almost lost it. Andre left her high and dry to be with another woman yet again.

She called her sugar daddy with the quickness who only took ten minutes to pick her up.

Tony was furious yet hurt when he saw Kameron sitting in the wheelchair in front of the hospital. He rushed out of his car, helping her into the front seat.

Closing the door back to her he couldn't wait until she told him what was going on. He had a million questions and wanted nothing more than answers.

Kameron palmed her face and the tears began. "I'm sorry baby I haven't called you but you can obviously see why I haven't called you. I told my husband about you and I asked for a divorce. From my understanding we were separated from some time now. As soon as I told him I was moving on, he went haywire on me." Kameron hysterically cried.

Leaning over towards her, Tony began massaging her shoulders. "I'm so sorry you have to go through this, I promise he'll never lay another finger on you again." Tony assured her.

Seeing Kameron there in such a wreck, his mind instantly went back to his daughters he couldn't imagine a man placing their hands on his baby girls. Had a man ever done so, they would indefinitely be meeting their maker sooner rather than later. One thing he couldn't tolerate was abusive no good having man.

Kameron had agreed to pack her things and move in with Tony. She felt as if she made the right decision. Andre and her were over with. She couldn't put up with his foul behavior. If Carmen or any other woman wanted him, they could have him…over her dead body.

"Baby, I'll see you in about an hour or so." Kameron spoke opening up the passenger door.

Tony hesitated then he reached over in his glove department, grabbing the cold steel and handed it to Kameron. "If that bastard ever put his hands on you again, you put him out of his misery. Do you hear me?" He told her.

With tears in her eyes, Kameron nodded her head in agreement. She leaned over and kissed him on the lips. "Thank you so much for everything baby. I'll be gone before he gets back." Kameron assured him.

A part of him wanted to stay until she was all packed and ready but she begged him to allow her to handle her sloppy mess and for him to stay clear of her drama. Respecting her wishes after she got in the house he pulled off and went back to clean up his home before his future arrived…

Kameron was a furious wreck. After tearing up the entire house, she didn't bother to call Andre. With the gun on her lap and a bottle of liquor turned up to her mouth she sat in a wooden rocking chair in front of the front door. Her free hand held onto the trigger tightly. Her devilish evil eyes were directly glued onto the door. Pure hatred and evilness were pumping through her veins, the only color she could see was red. Her mind was so alcohol and frustration induced that she had lost train of thought.

*****

Tony sped away not believing the shit that was taking place. Kameron was a good woman from what he could tell; she was just caught up in a bad marriage. Apparently it was an abusive one. He made a sharp turn to Carmen's house. He had to make sure that Carmen was alright. Something in his gut told him that his daughter had gotten caught up in some shit. He parked his car and hopped out. He was glad that he had a key so he made his way inside. He could hear crying coming from the back. He walked in her room to find her in a fetal position. Heart wrenching sobs filled the air and it alarmed Tony.

"Baby girl what's wrong?" Tony walked over and rubbed her back, causing her to flinch. He turned her over to find her face bruised and swollen.

"Who the fuck did this to you and please don't lie to me." Anger took over his body and mind.

"Nobody daddy, what are you doing here?" Carmen sat up looking at her father.

Tony looked at her a moment longer and didn't say anything. He sighed and ran his hands across his head. Carmen had gotten caught up in some shit and he was going to find out what the hell was going on. It had to be something because he never saw his daughter weak and broken.

"Daddy, just know that I'm not the perfect daughter that you thought I was. Sooner or later you will find out everything and I just hope nothing bad happens before then.

Chapter 20

Vic sat in his hotel room looking at all the pictures he had taken. He even had pictures of Carmen's and Keysha's father. Tony just didn't know that he was about to embark in a messy love triangle. Kameron was an old bitter hag that didn't give a fuck about nobody but herself. He almost felt sorry for Andre, but then again that's the thing of being a low down and dirty lover. He was fucking his wife's own daughter right under her nose. Since Vic had what he needed for right now, he was going to lay low, but first he had to send a little something to Tony. He was loving how all this was panning out.

Vic's brother was still in jail and that was a good thing. He had to have an opportunity with Keysha and was going to do so today. He had talked to her earlier and she was supposed to be coming to his lavish hotel. He was on his way back to his hotel room when he decided to follow the ambulance where he met Keysha waiting outside of the emergency room sobbing. At a little bit of soothing he was able to get her attention. The way Keysha looked at him, he knew she wanted to be loved. He could tell from the desperate look in her eyes that she wanted to be loved badly at that.

He had to make sure had everything put into a secure place before she arrived. Once he had everything squared away he stripped down and decided to take a shower. As he stood under the shower head his thoughts went to Keysha. She was sexy and was a freak. Vincent was just too stupid to see it. He obviously didn't know how to bring it out of her, but Vic was ready.

He hardened and he grabbed his shaft stroking back and forth. A loud knock brought him out of his lust filled haze.

Vic stopped the shower and wrapped a towel around his waist. He

Angel Williams & Lady Amethyst

walked to the door and Keysha stood there looking flawless and sexy as hell, even wearing the pair of sweat pants and top she had on. He pulled her inside, closing the door. Keysha nervously bit her lip as she stared into Vic's eyes. "Vic maybe I shouldn't be here." She grabbed the doorknob. Vic thought otherwise. She was an adult and accepting his invitation he knew she wanted to be there just as much as he wanted her there.

"Key, yes you should. Let me make you feel good. Let me relieve some stress." He picked her up placing her against the wall. He had no time to be beating around the bush. His dick was rock hard and he was tired of sexually pleasing himself. He wanted the real deal, which was Keysha. He could have had Nik as well and Kameron but the two didn't give him the sensation that appealed to him like Keysha did.

Key was so caught off guard, but turned on at the same time. He reached inside of her pants to find that she wasn't wearing panties. Vic smirked in satisfaction. "Damn Key, you knew you wanted the dick." He quickly turned her

Around, laying her on the king sized bed. He pulled her pants down and lifted her shirt off her body and growled in frank male appreciation. Spreading her thighs apart he blew on her erect clit. His tongue gave her one long lick as he looked into her eyes. He released his towel and his member aimed right for her dripping center. He fisted his shaft in his hand and moved the head up and down her wet slit. He tapped her clit, causing her to skeet a little bit.

"Damn Key." He spread her legs and eased his thickness inside.

He clenched his jaws because she was so tight and so wet. Her canal felt like it was never once attended too. He knew neither Vincent or Andre were pleasing her as a woman should have been pleased by the way her juices were flowing all in between her thighs and the way her eyes were rolling in the back of her head. He moved in and out of her in slow precision as she dug her nails in his back. He sped up, pounding inside of her. Her screams were loud and he had to drown out her screams by sliding his tongue in her mouth. He pulled out and made her get on all fours. He gripped her hair roughly and pushed up inside of her, showing her pussy no mercy. She gripped the cover as he fiercely pounded inside of her.

"Keysha tell me you love this dick?" He slapped her ass.

He glanced up in the corner noticing the red light was on the camera recording the sexual action that was going on. A part of him felt guilty for what he was doing. He didn't know rather it was the pussy or was he really growing a soft spot for Keysha.

"I-I-Fuck!" She screamed when she came long and hard.

"Damn I love the way I make you cum."

Vic continued his assault and finally he released hot semen inside her with a satisfied grunt. In that moment all Vic could think about was his brother was stupid and dumb as hell. Keysha's pussy now belonged to him and he knew that she would be coming back for more.

Chapter 21

Andre lay in the hospital bed looking at the ceiling; Keysha had left him a few hours ago and still hadn't got back yet. He couldn't believe how things had spun out of control. He had a feeling that what happened to him wasn't something that just happened, it was something that was staged. He could put money on that. He felt all alone like he had nobody. He couldn't call Nik because she was probably busy with her no good ass mother. At times like this he wished that his mother was there. The only remembrance he had of his mother was a picture that was placed safely underneath his mattress at home, a picture that he had got from his foster parents when he was ten years old. He didn't know where the hell his father was and at this point he could care less. He looked up when a nurse walked in. He glared at her and she smiled. At this point in his life he had nothing to smile about. His life was all fucked up.

"Dr. Fuller, how are you doing today?" The young nurse asked.

"How does it look like I'm doing?" He looked at her.

The nurse rolled her eyes and checked his IV. She made sure he was comfortable before she walked out. He had his cell phone with him and it rung. He looked down at the screen not recognizing the number. He decided to answer it.

"Hello."

"Andre, where the hell are you?"

"Carmen."

"Yeah it's me. Where the hell are you?"

"You mean to tell me you don't know?" He sighed in anger.

"No, what the hell is going on?" Carmen asked concerned.

"Carmen we really need to talk, but right now I'm in the hospital and I"

"Oh my God! Andre, what the hell happened? Are you okay?" She asked frantically.

"Carmen I'm not the man that I led you to believe I was. I have been sleeping with two other people and the one I was with last night their husband beat the living shit out of me."

Carmen didn't say anything. Hell she couldn't because she was sleeping around too with a few people which he now knew. She rolled her eyes, not that he had a wife but he had also been whoring around as well. She wanted to be angry, but she knew that she couldn't. "Listen when you are ready to be released, call me." Carmen said as she unlocked the door to her apartment. When she didn't want to be bothered with either Vincent or Andre or anyone else of that matter, she went back to her apartment. There were only a few people that knew she had the apartment.

"Okay and Carmen, I love you."

"I love you too."

*****

A knock sounded on her apartment door. She had no clue who was it could be because she had been trying her hardest to lay low. After her father left she thought about Andre because he was on her mind since the other day. Maybe what he wanted to do wasn't such a bad idea. She shook her thoughts away and opened the door to find Nik standing there. They stared at each other because it had been a while since they saw each other.

"Nik what are you doing here?" Carmen leaned into the doorjamb.

"I needed someone to talk to and you are the only one that I could talk to and at least trust. Can I come in?"

Carmen nodded and let her in. Once the door was closed Nik looked at Carmen's face. She lightly touched it and looked at her with questions in her eyes. "Carmen, what happened?"

"It's nothing." She held her head down and walked to her room.

"What do you mean it's nothing?" Nik yelled.

Carmen looked at her and got lost in her eyes. It was something so pure and innocent like with Nik. That was one of the reasons that she was attracted to her. Carmen had never been with another woman until she met Nik, it was first supposed to be just a little friendly outing. After a few drinks, one thing led to another and here they were, mixed in a dangerous love triangle. They were once upfront and honest with one another, now everything they started to build, was built upon lies after lies, adultery and dangerous liaisons. The love triangle was messy and very dangerous.

Carmen smoothed Nik's hair back and captured her lips in a heart stopping kiss. Nik slid her hands down to Carmen's butt and squeezed. Nik pulled back and remembered that she really came to talk not to have sex.

"Carmen as bad as I want to I can't. I came to talk to you about my mother."

"What's going on with your mother?" Carmen asked as she rubbed up and down Nik's sides.

Nik couldn't think straight with her touching her. It was something about her touch. Nik closed her eyes as Carmen trailed kisses down the column of her neck. Nik felt her leggings being slid down and she knew it was no use in fighting the temptation. Clothes came off in a blur as they tongued each other down. Carmen worshiped Nik's body and made her cum over and over again as her tongue made love to her slick folds. She would just have to tell Carmen about Kameron later, right now she just needed to be loved.

Chapter 22

Tony sat behind his desk as he looked at the letter that came from his attorney. He didn't know what to make of the information that he had just gotten. He had a son, a son that had been in the system for many years.

He was now a big time doctor at Lancaster Memorial. Andre Fuller was twenty-nine years old and he was doing well. He was married, but he didn't know who he was married to. That piqued his curiosity. It was too many secrets and Tony didn't like that. Tony folded the information back into the envelope and stared out his window. His thoughts strayed to Kameron and the messy situation she was in with her husband. Tony felt that it was something more that she wasn't telling him, but things would surely come to the light soon.

He had talked to Kameron earlier and she didn't sound like herself. Something was off with her and he had to go find out what the hell was going on, but first he had to go see Keysha. That's who he hadn't seen or talked to. He stood and was making his way out of his office when his doorbell sounded. He went to the door and opened it.

"Are you Tony Fuller?" The courier asked.

"Yes I am."

"Well these are for you." The manila envelope was pushed into his hand.

Tony looked down in confusion. He looked around and closed the door. He took a seat on his plush leather sofa and opened the envelope. He dumped the contents out and what he saw brought rage to him. There before his eyes were pictures of Kameron sucking and riding Vincent's dick. Tony stood up and slung the pictures on the floor. "That bitch was trying to play me for a fool. Sleeping with my daughter's husband and crying to me." He said aloud.

Tony knew what he was going to do and it wasn't going to be pretty, but it was time to let motherfuckers know Tony Fuller wasn't to be played with or his family. He picked up the phone and called Carmen.

"Hello daddy." She answered groggily.

"I need you to meet me somewhere in fifteen." He barked.

"Daddy what's going on?" She eased out of bed so that she wouldn't wake Nik.

"I have some shit to show you and it's about your sister's husband."

Carmen's heart lurched and her hand trembled as she held the phone. She didn't know what the hell was going on, but she feared that it was something bad. She quickly prayed that her dad didn't find out the dirt that she was doing.

Being that he was cursing and talking in a loud tone rather than his normal mild tone she knew he was upset and it had to be something serious.

"Okay daddy where do you want to meet?"

"In the parking lot of the corner market." He disconnected the call.

All he could see was red. Tony couldn't believe how Kameron had played him. Payback was a real bitch.

*****

Nik looked up when she saw that Carmen was fully dressed. "Where are you going?"

She asked as he folded her arms across her bare breast.

"I have to go take care of something. Just go back to sleep and I promise I will be right back." Carmen reassured her.

"Carmen there is something I need to tell you before you go." Nik bit down on her lip.

"What is it? I really have to go." Carmen looked aggravated.

"It's about my mother. She has fallen off the deep end. All she does is drink and talk to herself. She isn't the same anymore. She talks about always competing with young bitches." Nik dropped her head in shame.

"Nik what are you telling me?" Carmen narrowed her eyes. Nik was always talking about her mom, it was as if she idolized her or something. Carmen was fed up hearing about Nik's momma.

"Carmen I have been sleeping with my mother's husband. He took my virginity and all. He keeps me laced in the finest shit and all I have to do is fuck him whenever he wants. This has been going on since I moved here, right in their house. If he knew I was fucking with you he would be livid. He told me that my pussy only belonged to him and no other man, but he didn't say I couldn't share it with a woman."

Carmen narrowed her eyes. She felt a since of relief that she had finally got it off her chest. She been dying for so long to tell someone what was going on between the walls of her mother's home. Carmen was the only person who she could trust to share the information with, because at the end of the day she knew she was just as guilty as Andre was.

"Did you tell anyone else this?" Carmen asked Nik.

Nik bit her bottom lip. "No, you are the only person I trust. If I tell someone and—"

Carmen quickly cut her off as she attend to her ringing phone. She quickly answered it on the half of the ring,

"Keysha where are you?" She gasped.

Hearing the mention of Keysha's name, Nik laid back in the bed with her face dug into the pillow. She felt like every time she tried to talk to Carmen it was always something.

"I'm in my car about to head home." Carmen could hear it in her voice that she was somewhat happy. She didn't sound down and depressed like she had been sounding like a few days ago.

"Are you okay?" She asked her sister.

"Oh yeah, I'm real good. Are you good?" Keysha asked as she thought about Vic. It wasn't just the sex, it was more than sex. Her heart was telling her so. Regardless she couldn't get Vic off her mind.

"Why are you so happy?" Carmen asked.

"Life is getting so much better for me." Keysha smiled.

Her line began beeping and she looked at the familiar name that was calling on the other line. A smile crept across her face as she thought that she was actually being thought about.

"Hey, let me call you back. Love you." Keysha cheerfully spoke and clicked over on the other line.

Carmen gathered her things and before leaving the apartment she kissed Nik on the forehead.

"Hello." Keysha answered in a soft voice. Vic was throbbing yet again at the sound of her voice.

"Hey, I was thinking, before you left it was rude of me to ask if you

91

ate today?"

Keysha chuckled a bit, she could tell that Vic was a bit nervous. Keysha thought for a second and her mind was already made up. Vic was pursuing her and seemed like he was interested and that gave her enough ammunition to pursue him back.

"Actually Vic, I didn't eat. I'm on my way back to you now. I'll see you in a few." She said.

Vic stared at the phone for a second. He was all smiles. "Oh alright." He replied before hanging up.

Low Down & Dirty Lovers

Chapter 23

Keysha made it back to Vic's hotel in a matter of ten minutes. She honked the horn and patiently waited for him to come out.

"Where are we going?" He asked getting into the car.

"Let's just grab something quick and come back here and eat." She told him.

He stopped and thought for a second. "Do you like seafood?" He asked.

"I love seafood." Keysha smiled.

"Then get in the passenger seat, I have a great carryout in mind." He told her.

Keysha hopped out of the car with the quickness like a teenage girl who was in lust with the crush of her life.

The two of them met each other at the rear of the car. Vic reached out grabbing her face and slid his tongue in her mouth. As their tongues danced to a beat that the only the two of them heard it was like fireworks exploding in their hearts and in their midsections. The connection the two of them had was magically unexplainable.

Standing back Vic stared into Keysha's eyes. He could now feel why at one point of time why Vincent was so in love with her. How couldn't one be? She was everything a man ever wanted and ever dreamed of. She was sweet, heavenly beautiful and also smart as a whip. Just when it came to Vincent her vision was quiet blurred which made her at times look as if she wasn't the smartest one in the bunch. It was so odd how one being can make another look so dumb.

Their eyes locked and was fixed on one another's for a few seconds. "Let's go get this food." Vic told Keysha. She nodded her head agreeing, walking to the passenger seat.

94

Vic only came in town for one reason and one reason only. He hated that he couldn't control himself nor his heart when he was around Keysha.

Driving thirty minutes out, the two of them shared great conversation. Keysha was able to open up to Vic about any and almost everything. She was even able to tell him about Andre and almost slipped up and told him about a secret that she vowed to take to her grave.

Vic's welcoming demeanor almost had her telling on herself.

After they got their food they made their way back to his hotel. They ate, shared laughs and in a matter of minutes the two of them were back out of their clothing.

Vic watched with his lustful eyes in satisfaction as Keysha sucked him. He gripped her hair as she swallowed all nine inches like a pro. He felt his nut fast approaching. He pulled out of her warm wet mouth and pushed her back on the bed. He wanted to release inside of her. He intended to leave a mark, a nine month mark. This would surely teach his whack ass brother a lesson. He got satisfaction in knowing that she had stopped taking birth control a few weeks ago. Keysha had confided in Vic telling him that she wanted a baby so bad, but Vincent didn't want one right now. That was music to Vic's ears because he would gladly give her what she wanted.

"Fuck, Key!" He stroked harder and faster.

"Shit, Vic I'm cumming!" She screamed as her cream coated Vic's shaft.

Keysha didn't care about anything anymore although she was worried about Andre and hoped that he was okay, especially after the way Vincent had beat him up.

"Tell me you want to have my baby!" Vic demanded.

Keysha didn't give it any thought. He was stroking her so damn good, she wanted to cry in fact she did cry out. "Vic, I want to have your baby! Ohhhhh God!"

Vic growled as her came inside her for the fourth time. He eased out of her and pulled her up. He kissed her passionately feeling shit that he didn't need to feel. This wasn't about love, this was about revenge and revenge only.

Angel Williams & Lady Amethyst

Chapter 24

Carmen's heart raced when her dad pulled out the envelope. He handed it to her. She slowly opened it, her heart pace sped up. Sweat began to form on her forehead as she began to sweat profusely. The palm of her hands began to excessively sweat, her stomach growled with bubble guts. She turned to her dad and he was still piercing her soul with his eyes, wearing a mean expression on his face. She took out the pictures and sighed when she saw Vincent and Kameron. She was shocked and surprise, but was more thankful that she hadn't got caught. She thought back to the pictures she had and it was obvious that she was being watched, now Vincent was being watched. She thought about if Keysha had hired a private investigator. That was something she was more than sure she was going to ask her sister about.

She thought about her sister, had she found out the truth about things? She thought about would it be better if she told her or if she allowed someone to send Keysha pictures. She made her mind up, she had to get herself right. Admitting was the first step. Being the bigger person she was going to woman up, put her big girl panties on and tell her sister the low down about her and her husband.

Carmen turned and faced her angry dad, "Dad I should have been told you that they were having ongoing issues for some time now. But Keysha made me promise not to tell you. I'm going to take this to her and have a talk with her.

I think it's best if she hears and see this in my presence and not yours."

Tony nodded his head agreeing, "This whole situation upsets me not solely because what Vincent did to my daughter, but also because that bitch in the picture is the woman who I fell in love with. The woman who is supposed to be moving into my home later today." Tony spoke as his heart cried with anger.

Carmen gasped and covered her mouth, "Daddy, please believe me you can do so much better than this female." She spoke pointing at the picture. She desperately wanted to tell her dad she knew exactly who Kameron was but decided against it.

Tony shook his head agreeing, no matter how much he tried to convince himself, he still had feelings for Kameron.

She was human just like everyone else. He was going to give her another chance of being honest with him and if she was, then he was going to forgive her.

"Okay daddy, I'm going to go talk to Keysha now. I'll call you later to let you know how things went."

Tony nodded his head as he reached out giving his daughter a bear hug, "Hey Carmen, just remember that you don't ever have to settle for any men like Vincent. You or Keysha don't have to. It's so many good men out there in this world today."

Carmen nodded. "I know daddy and I won't so you don't have to worry about that." She kissed him on the forehead and slid out of the car.

When Carmen got back to her car, she called Keysha.

"Hello." Keysha spoke in a soft voice, trying not to wake Vic.

"Hey sis, meet me at your house. I need to talk to you for a minute."

Keysha looked at Vic who was just opening his eyes, then back at the phone. "Is it important?" She questioned.

"Yes it is. It's very important so please meet me there." She told her.

Keysha looked over at Vic again and then back at the phone. She was torn between the two. Vic heard everything over the phone. He nodded his head to her.

"Okay, I'll be there in thirty minutes." Keysha told Carmen.

"See you then." Carmen spoke.

Keysha didn't want to but she eased out of bed and put her clothes on. Vic sat up in bed and thought for a few seconds. "Bring all of your shit back here." He told her.

"What?" Keysha raised her eyebrow.

"I'm not taking no for an answer. I want you with me. Bring all of your shit back."

Keysha stared at him and smiled. Although things were going bad with Vincent in her she had to think about reality first. He was her sponsor. She was a stay at home wife, she couldn't leave her home to be laid up in a hotel with a man. Little did she know, Vic was there to only take care of business. Back in Richmond, Virginia his life was a complete different story. He could offer her everything and then some, more than what his brother was offering her. Besides the materialistic things, he could offer his heart, his honesty and loyalty, which was very well priceless.

Three years after Vincent had put him out, he was contacted by a lawyer where he was rewarded a $300,000 that their mom had left him. It could have possibly came from their dad Victor Sr. Their mom was famous for taking money from Victor and saving it, she always said just in case it was an emergency but he never questioned it. Instead he took the money and considered it as a blessing.

Keysha kissed Vic and left the hotel. Twenty minutes later she was pulling up at her house.

*****

Carmen had just made it to Keysha's house. She noticed Keysha car was already parked outside. She was just ready to step out when her phone began ringing. She scrunched her nose up at the four digit number.

"Hello, who is this?" She said and was directly speaking with an answering service.

She frowned her face up, just as she was about to hang up she heard Vincent voice.

"Hey Carmen I need a big favor." Vincent said over the phone.

Carmen rolled her eyes. She already knew that Vincent and Andre had gotten in to it. "What do you need Vincent?"

"I need you to come bail me out. I'm in prison I can't be here."

"Why can't you be there?" Carmen curiously asked.

"It's bad for my reputation, how can I represent criminals if I'm behind bars myself. This just don't look good." He spoke.

Carmen laughed to herself, "Is it that Vincent or are you afraid to be there?"

Vincent banged his fist against the wall, he was getting irritated with Carmen taunting him by the second.

"Just come bail me the fuck out now!" Vincent roared.

"Why can't your daddy come bail you out?" Carmen sucked her

99

teeth.

Vincent hated that he had called Carmen. Had his father been back from his two month vacation from Europe, he would have had been got his precious son out of jail.

"He's not in the states." Vincent huffed.

"Oh, I see. Did you call Keysha, *your wife*?" Carmen smiled.

Vincent was fuming. He had called Keysha numerous of times and she yet to answer the phone for him. He had something for her ass once he got out. If she thought what he did to Andre was something, if she knew what was best for her, she would run and run far away at that.

No matter what the situation was, Vincent felt like Keysha was supposed to be his wife. No matter what she was supposed to have his back and was supposed to have been bailed him out.

"Look can you or can't you?" Vincent huffed.

Carmen laughed to herself again. She thought about how Vincent left her high and dry when she had got ran over months back. She reached out to him on numerous of occasions yet he never got back with her. To make matters even worse, he went far beyond measures of avoiding any contact with her.

"Yeah, I'll be there in an hour." She lied.

"Thank you so much baby, I love you. I promise you things will be right with us." He told her, willing to tell her just about anything so she could come get his scary ass out of jail before some mad inmate make a mockery out of his ass.

Carmen hung the phone up, the last thing on her mind was bailing Vincent out.

She killed the ignition to her car and climbed out the car.

"Hey Keysha." Carmen said to her sister giving her a hug.

"Hey sis," Keysha returned the gesture.

Carmen took one look at her sister and noticed that her sister was very joyful. "Why are you in such a good mood?" Carmen asked Keysha.

Keysha sighed then a wide smile was painted across her face. "I met a man. And oh my gosh, Carmen! I'm so into him!"

Keysha went on and on telling Carmen about Vic. Carmen sat there and listened, a part of her was happy for her sister while the other part of her was envious. How could her sister always manage to find love and a good man, yet she was always playing somebodies side chick?

What was she doing wrong? What did Keysha have that she didn't have?

"I'm so happy for you. But Keysha I don't want to rain on your parade but these were delivered to daddy." Carmen spoke, sliding the envelope out of her handbag.

Keysha kept yapping as she took the envelope and opened it. Seeing the pictures of her husband, she was speechless.

Although she was really feeling Vincent she was speechless and hurt at the same time. She took her thumb, wiping the tears away from the corner of her eyes.

She then thought back about Vic who told her to bring all her belongings back. She was tired of Vincent and was going to give him a taste of his own medicine for once and all.

She was tired of being hurt and tired of all the ones around her who claimed to love her and hurt her too. Even Carmen!

"Can you do me a favor?" Keysha asked Carmen.

Carmen nodded her head, "What is it?"

"I'm leaving Vincent today. Please help me pack some things. I want to be gone by the time he gets home."

"I'll help you pack, but I hope you are not running off with that guy that you barely know. He could be dangerous for all that you know."

Keysha shook her head, "I'm not running off with no one. I'm running away from my no good husband before he gets back. I haven't bailed him out yet, so I know it's going to be trouble when he gets back."

Carmen understood. She thought it was best for Keysha to leave Vincent, why not continue to kick him while he was down and out? He did deserve everything that was coming to him after all.

Keysha and Carmen packed five duffle bags, containing important papers, shoes, clothing and her expensive handbags and jewelry. After taking everything to the car Keysha looked back at the house that she once shared with her husband, who she thought she was going to spend forever and forever with.

She turned to Carmen with tears rolling down her face. Carmen hugged her baby sister tightly. "Everything is going to be okay." She assured her sister. She wanted to tell Keysha about her and Vincent yet she decided that now was not the time.

Keysha stared at her sister with sad puppy eyes. "Burn this house down! I want Vincent to really feel my pain."

A guilty Carmen did as her sister told. She went back into the house and gathered a can of gas from the garage, turned the gas stove on, and in a matter of seconds she rushed out the front door.

A smile crept across Keysha's face when she saw the house go up in flames in broad daylight. She didn't care if the neighbors caught site of what was going on or whatnot. Before any of them saw what Carmen had just done, they pulled off and went in separate directions.

Keysha headed to the bank, Carmen headed back to her apartment.

An hour later, Keysha was walking out the bank; she had just wiped Vincent bank account dry. Leaving nothing behind but a single nickel… A nickel for his thoughts, next time before he crossed her, or any other female who gave him her heart he would think twice. Karma wasn't a bitch, Keysha was a BITCH, who anyone dared to cross her better watch out for.

Low Down & Dirty Lovers

Chapter 25

Tony was just about to go home as he passed by the hospital. Then he thought about the letter that was delivered to him. He thought twice before pulling into the parking lot of the hospital. It was better now than later. He couldn't believe that he had a son that he had with his Marissa. She had gotten pregnant at the age of fifteen and had the baby when she was sixteen. She was moved away after that, which is why he didn't know about his son. He was grateful for his attorney getting him this information. He sat in the parking lot thinking about all the good times that he and Marissa had. They were specially made for one another, when they exchanged vows, until death did the two of them a part. Through sickness and health, loving his wife he stood by her side. Every doctor's appointment she had, he made sure his schedule was free so he could attend. She wanted her dream house; he made sure she had it. She wanted the finer things out of life; he made sure he gave her those. He was her sun and she was his shine, magically together the two of them brought sunshine into their lives and others as well.

He wished that he could find a woman like her now, but women were so scandalous these days. It was obvious that Marissa was one of a kind; he had to soon realize to let go and let bygones and bygones. Marissa wasn't easy *imitated* and could never be *duplicated*. Tony still had some questions as to how is Andre's last name was Fuller. He figured that going in here he would get all the information that he needed.

Tony stepped out of his car and made his way inside the hospital. He walked in and looked around. He approached the nurse's station. "Excuse me, but can you point me in the direction of Andre Fuller?"

"Yes he is in room 312." The nurse smiled.

Tony nodded and walked in the direction the nurse indicated. Before he walked in he took a deep breath. This was all new to him. He was used to just having daughters, but now having a son made a difference. He thought about turning around for a split second, wondering if it was too late to now be in his son's life. Then he reckoned that it was always better to be soon or now rather than never.

He finally pushed the door open and Andre was sitting up in the bed looking at a file. He looked so much like his mother and nothing like him.

Tony cleared his throat and Andre looked up. He had no real clue who this man was, but it was obvious that he knew him or at least he thought he knew him.

"Can I help you with something?" Andre looked at the stranger.

"I believe you can." Tony walked further into the room and took seat.

Andre closed the file and looked at the man, wondering what the hell was up. The days that he had been here nobody came to see him and he wondered why this man was here now.

"What is it that you think I can help you with?" Andre focused his attention on him.

"Where do I begin?" Tony looked down and back up to Andre.

Andre looked at him and wondered what was up with him. He kind of looked distraught. He actually looked like he felt. Andre's life was a like a living hell. During his time in the hospital he had time to think. He thought of his mother and how he wished that she was here. He even wished that he knew who his father was.

"Andre, do you remember a woman named Marissa Chambers?"

He furrowed his eyebrows as he looked at the man who had yet identified himself.

"First tell me who the hell you are." Andre folded his arms across his chest. He wasn't going to take no shit from anyone. Although he was dishing out all of this bullshit he sure as hell didn't plan on taking any of it back.

"Andre, I'm Tony Fuller your father."

Andre looked at him and thought that his hearing was failing him. He had just thought to himself before he arrived, saying that he wished he knew who his father was. This couldn't actually be happening. Things like this just didn't happen, did they?

"Listen I already have enough going on in my life for you to be coming in here playing games with me." Andre yelled.

"Andre I understand your frustration, but I'm not one to play games. Your mother and I had a good life. We were young and in love. Her parents sent her away one day and I never knew why. I thought that I had done something wrong, but I was told that she had to go away for a while. I was hurt and confused. When she did return, things seem strained and I felt like she had a secret that was eating her alive. She never mentioned having a baby."

Andre listened and he knew that he wasn't lying because his mother wrote to him every day while living with his great aunt who was his foster mother that he barely knew. Until the day she died he still didn't know who she was.

Everything felt like a mystery being they were so secretive. When he turned fourteen his birthday present was an oversized box filled with letters from his biological mother. She hated leaving him behind, but she had no choice in the matter. Back then it wasn't okay for a woman that young to have a baby out of wedlock.

"So I guess you are wondering how my last name if Fuller since my mother wasn't married to you then." Andre looked at him.

"Yes I am."

"Well my aunt Grace named me and since she was a Fuller I inherited the name." He shrugged as if it were no big deal. Tony was somewhat thrilled that Tony had inherited the Fuller's last name, being that both of his daughters went by the last name of Jones. Which was their mother's maiden name.

"So I'm guessing that you don't have kids." Tony questioned.

"No I believe I married the wrong woman to be having kids with, but that's a whole other story."

Tony nodded and wondered what he meant by that. Right now he would leave that alone. His focus was on getting to know his son after all this time.

Low Down & Dirty Lovers

Chapter 26

Two days had passed and Tony took Andre home with him. He even got him a personal nurse to aid him until he was able to get back on his feet. Tony had learned a lot in talking with Andre. He still was closed off about parts of his life. Tony understood that because it was hard to trust someone especially someone that had just popped up out of nowhere. Tony walked downstairs to where Andre was. He was sitting in a chair out in the sunroom. He stared at the fountain outback. Tony watched him for a while, but decided not to bother him.

"Nurse Tina make sure you take good care of him." Tony told her.

"I certainly will, Mr. Fuller. He is in good hands with me." She smiled brightly.

Tony walked out to go attend to some important business matters.

****

Andre heard the door to the sun room open and the nurse that his father had hired stepped inside. He watched as she busied herself getting his medicine ready. He couldn't help but notice how pretty and thick the nurse was. She pranced around in her leggings and a t-shirt that said Nurses Rock. Her long hair was parted in the center and hung down her back. Her slanted eyes were hypnotic and the hazel color made them exotic. He felt his shaft stiffen as he watched her butt jiggle every time she moved.

He desperately yearned the touch of a woman. He hadn't had any pussy in days from any of the women in his life who ran out on him when he was down.

She turned and headed in his direction with the medicine and bottled water. She flashed her dimpled grin and Andre couldn't help but smile back. She passed the medicine and water to him. Andre didn't take his eyes off of her as he took his pain medicine and drank his water.

"Can I get you anything else?" Tina asked as she looked down at his thick erection showing through his basketball shorts.

Andre smiled because he saw where her attention had gone and could use a good nut right about now. "There is one thing you can do for me." He reached for her wrist.

"What's that?" She bit on her lip.

"Some sexual pleasure." He pulled her in front of him.

"What do you need or better yet what would you like?" She reached down and caressed his erection.

Tina was more than a freak, all of her clients, she surely help *nurse* them back to good health with sexual pleasures.

He smiled and pulled himself out of his shorts. She eased her leggings and thong down, easing onto his thick tool. They both groaned in satisfaction as she moved up and down on him slowly. He gripped her waist helping to guide her movements. She felt so good and she was so wet.

"Damn Tina!" He grunted when she clamped her walls around him

He felt himself about to release and so did Tina because she hopped of him and dropped down taking him into her mouth. She sucked him until she had gotten every drop. She fixed her clothes and she placed his member back inside his shorts.

"Is there anything else that I can get you, Andre?"

"No that will be all for now." He said wearing a smile of satisfaction.

"Okay let me know if you do need anything and I do mean *anything*." She said as she strutted off.

Andre sat back and thought life was actually looking up and that wasn't the only thing that was up...

******

Vic was satisfied with the way everything was going. He still had some things up his sleeves, but he was lying low for now. He had Keysha back in his arms and he didn't want to do anything to lose her, until he made sure she was his for sure and wasn't going anywhere. He learned from his brother first hand, what to do to keep her happy and what not to do to drive her into the arms of another man.

He couldn't wait for Vincent to find out about him being there, but first there were some other things that he needed to wrap up. Things were going better than he expected and he was sitting back laughing at it all. Vincent and Vic never had a good relationship. They tried to pretend as if they did but the two of them knew better. Vic always felt like the outcast, but all that was changing now. Vic held all the power and he knew what to do with it.

Now that Tony knew that Andre was his son he couldn't wait for the big explosion to take place. Everybody thought that the next person could be trusted, but in this game that wasn't the case. Vic looked out of his hotel window and just watched the traffic as he milled about. Life was finally looking up in more ways than one.

Chapter 27

Vincent sat in the jail cell fuming. He had been played and he was sure to kill some fucking body whenever he got out. He thought about all the drama and dirt he did. He now felt like karma was staring him in the face. His name was going to be carried through the mud because he was a public official that represented clients such as him. He couldn't believe how the tables had turned on him. He chuckled to himself because this was unbelievable. He looked around at as the prison guards moved about with inmates. Vincent didn't belong here and he had to get out of here one way or the other.

Since he had been locked up he had this one guard that was fine as hell that would hook him up with head from time to time. That was a plus. He knew that him being a criminal attorney that also handles divorce cases wasn't a good thing, considering where he was. He had to get out of there some way. He just prayed that someone would take mercy on him and get him out. At this point he didn't care who it was as long as he got out. He held his head down when he heard his name being called.

"Vincent Wiggler." One of the guards yelled.

He looked up and waited for him to say what he needed to say.

"Somebody just posted your bail. You are free to go." He opened the cell letting Vincent walk out.

Vincent walked out getting his belongings from lockup. When he rounded the corner he stopped in his tracks when he saw who was waiting for him as well as bailed him out. Vincent smiled and knew that things were really looking up.

Chapter 28

Andre sat back and his mind went back to Kameron, she was his wife after all. Although they had their ups and downs as every other relationship, he decided that he needed to come clean with her about everything, all expect about Nik. But the others he felt that she should know about. Maybe she could get a better understand why if he told her about the emptiness that he was feeling every day of his life. Regardless he felt like he should come clean as well as tell her that he wanted a divorce. What they had was broken and deranged love and there was no repairing it.

"Tina." Andre called out.

Tina poked her head in the door frame. "Yes." She softly spoke.

Andre turned facing her and smiled. She was so gorgeous and sexy that he couldn't help but harden in his pants.

"I do need a favor, I been in here for two days. I need a bit of fresh air." Andre told her.

Tina shook her head agreeing.

Andre didn't want Tina know exactly where he was going so he got dropped off two blocks away from his home.

"I'll call you in about an hour to come back for me." He told Tina.

She shook her head agreeing, "Be careful. Had I known you were going out to be walking around I would have never brought you outside." Tina told him before pulling off.

Andre shook his head and waived her off as he waited for her to pull off.

Once she disappeared around the corner he slowly began walking towards the direction of his house. Through the pain that he was in, he kept going. It was a must that he ended things with Kameron the right way.

******

Tony called Kameron phone for about four times before he decided to drive in the direction of her home. He thought about life and life was too short. Then he thought about the situation that Kameron was in, her husband had already beaten her badly, and if he could do anything to save her then he was going to do so. Whether they were together or not. The lies she told, still wouldn't allow him to have a cold heart towards her, plus he honestly didn't know the truth. All that matter to him was that he wouldn't be able to sleep at night had something happen to her. Then he kept thinking about his daughters if someone was able to save them, he would like if they saved them rather than leaving them in a dangerous situation which could turn into a deadly situation within the blink of an eye.

Then he thought about the gun he had given Kameron for her protection. If anything went left, he could possibly be the one going down as well, because it was his gun after all.

By the time he headed to Kameron's house the sun had just went away. Turning off his car, he got out.

******

Low Down & Dirty Lovers

Drunken, Kameron had waited over an hour for Andre to arrive. An hour turned into two whole damn days. She rocked back and forth as she took deep swigs of the alcohol. She felt like a maniac, she started talking to herself. Answering herself and questioning herself. The drama over the prior weeks had drove her insane. She didn't know rather she was coming or going. The song that was playing non-stop was on repeat and it began playing again. Kameron began singing with a broken voice and a broken heart.

"While all the time that I was loving you

You were busy loving yourself

I would stop breathing if you told me to

Now you're busy loving someone else

Eleven years out of my life

Besides the kids I have nothing to show

Wasted my years a fool of a wife

I shoulda have left your ass long time ago

Well I'm not gon cry,

I'm not gon cry,

I'm not gon shed no tears

No, I'm not gon cry,

it's not the time

cuz you're not worth my tears

Well I'm not gon cry,

I'm not gon cry,

I'm not gon shed no tears

No, I'm not gon cry,

it's not the time,

cuz you're not worth my tears"

Her eyes darted at the front door, at the sound of hearing the door knob turning. It was now dark outside and dark inside of the house. She had failed to get up to turn on any lights. In fact she had been sitting here the entire time, the only time she got up was to use the bathroom or to get her another bottle of alcohol from out the kitchen. She grabbed the gun, tightly gripping it with all of her power. As she thought about what she was about to do, tears ran down her cheeks. Her hands began to roughly shake a bit. Putting her bottle of Vodka down, she was able to subside the shaking of her hands and was able to grip the gun with both hands now. Her heart was now just as cold and dark as it was outside. If not even colder and darker.

The door came swinging open.

POW! The gun screamed a furious scream of death. The powerful kick behind the gun sent Kameron thin frame flying backwards out of the chair. The chair was steady rocking as the bullet ripped through its victim's chest.

"Ahhh!" They cried out in pure agony. The pain shot throughout their body like a bat out of hell. The excruciating pain drove them nearly into a coma. Their body violently shook fearfully.

Kameron jumped to her feet. Tears strolled down her face, she then realized that she made a terrible mistake. It was a total accident. "Oh my God baby, I'm so sorry." She cried, dropping to her knees she tried to stop the blood that was crazy over flowing, blood was everywhere. "Oh God! Oh God!" She frantically shook with a mixture of hurt and fear.

Her tonsils trembled as she violently screamed out in agony; her scream pierced the ears of her visitor that was just knocking on her door. It was so heart wrenching and powerful.

Their eyes locked for a long second, Kameron watch as the love of her life chest heaved up and down, soon nearing their last breath.

The links and chains were connected only to break one by one. Things were about to spin way out of control and there was nothing that neither of these low down and dirty lovers could do…

To Be Continued

Hell Between My Thighs

Chasity's Storm

A Novel By Angel Williams

Intro

It was a cold and weary Sunday morning, too damn cold to be summer in New Jersey. I sat up in my Princess canopy bed against my pink and purple princess sheets. My princess bed was made like a Cinderella carriage. Daddy said it was fit for a Princess such as I. The top poles were draped with a sheer pink sheet that hung near the floor. When I was in my bed, under the sheets, I felt protected.

My mind was all over the place as I thought about what happened the night before. The only things I could remember were the screams and cries that came from my own mouth. I begged and pleaded for the fat bastard to stop, but he didn't. He continued to pound hard and harder at my insides like there was no tomorrow, having no sort of mercy on my innocent young body. The thought of the agony and the abuse sent chills crawling up my spine.

I gripped the sheets and squeezed my legs tight as the pain lingered in my insides. I hated that my father had to work so damn late and couldn't protect me from the beast, or the beast who allowed the beast to do so many hurtful things to me.

"Please stop. I don't want to do this." I had cried and scratched at his fat back as I   tried to get him to stop.

My eyes locked with his and I saw that he wasn't concerned with my agony. He had his eyes on the prize and that's all he wanted. Our eyes met again and I pleaded with him, complete with sorrowful eyes and poked out lips. But that did no good, all he saw was a pretty young thing filled with purity. Or so he thought. Little did he know, I was innocent in the eyes of others, but it was far from the truth. I was consumed with guilt as he dug deep in my canal. This fruit was supposed to only belong to my love. I couldn't risk him finding out and look at me as a failure for breaking the promise that we swore on…

My bedroom door cracked open and the wooden floor creaked as JoeLee tiptoed into my room, got in bed and lay next to me.

JoeLee was three years older than I was but very sensitive. Look at JoeLee the wrong way and tears would start. JoeLee was softer than cotton candy. I wrapped my arms around him.

"Shhh, stop crying. Everything is going to be okay," I assured.

Unbeknownst to us, this would be the day that my daddy finally got fed up with Vera and her scandalous ways.

Over the loud arguments and JoeLee's nonstop cries, we could still hear the rain as it thumped against my windowpane.

"I'm tired of you and all of your shit. I go to work to come back and find different men in my damn house!" My daddy roared.

"Play your part and I won't have to bring men home," Vera screamed at the top of her lungs. "Play your GOT DAMN PART!"

I always wanted my daddy to grow enough balls to confront Vera and put a stop to her adultery. All the years I wanted him to have balls, I never realized that my daddy had to have humongous balls to put up with Vera and her mess.

SLAP! SLAP! SLAP!

"Don't you talk to me like that, you damn whore! My mother always told me you couldn't turn a whore into a housewife!"

"You damn pervert, I know all your dirty little secrets! What makes you think you are better than me? You are just like me and I'm just like you!" Vera said to my father as her eyes pierced his.

That's right, Daddy, beat that bitch ass! My insides screamed as I heard Vera cry out for help.

I couldn't sit in bed and hold JoeLee any longer. I had to witness this for myself. Never had Daddy put his hands on Vera before, although she had deserved a physical beating for years.

My daddy was a good man, a damn good man at that. I love him with everything in me. He was the only one in the world who was able to love me like no other and make me feel *special,* how every princess should feel.

Vera walked all over him. She ran a prostitution ring in our home while he worked fourteen hard hours a day. As much as my daddy pretended not to know what went on, I knew he had to know. How couldn't he have known? I know the rumors circulated around town like a hay fire, and sure didn't miss him one bit. Yet, I didn't hate him, I could never hate him.

"Don't you dare put your hands on me, you damn coward!" Vera cried as she held the side of her face.

I wondered what the hell she did with Miss Billy Badass. Every other time she wanted to jump bad, now she was crying like a damn wuss.

Daddy grabbed her by her throat and rammed her head into the wall, the imprint of Vera's head behind.

This was the most excitement I'd had in the thirteen years of my life. My heart raced as my eyes lit up with excitement.

I admired my daddy so much. He always taught JoeLee not to hit females because that showed cowardice, but I didn't see nothing wrong with him beating Vera's ass. He was far from a coward; in fact, in my eyes he was my *hero*.

"Beat her ass!" I got beside myself and cheered Daddy on.

Daddy's pride had been walked on countless times; his kindness was mistaken for weakness. And one thing you never do is mess with a man's ego. Vera had ripped his manhood from him the day she decided to bring a man into his home and sex him for a duece duece and forty bucks. She was so careless that she even had sex in her and Daddy's bed, leaving the scent of cheap sex behind for Daddy to smell later after a hard day of work.

Daddy beat the brakes off Vera for at least twenty minutes straight.

I watched with big eyes and enjoyed every second of it. JoeLee and I both ignored her as she begged us to call 911. The only thing that stopped him was when the neighbors knocked on the door and threatened to call the police. *Only in Jersey do you find super save a hoe folks,* I thought to myself.

My smile turned into a slight frown when my daddy gave Vera one last kick in the ass that sent her flying to the next room. Then he went into the bedroom they shared and grabbed a suitcase full of his things.

"Please don't leave me, I love you." Vera sobbed as she lay on the floor balled up in a fetal position.

I think reality had finally kicked in for her, but now it was way too late. "I promise you I will get some help for my illness," she cried. She tried to take the easy way out. Blame all her scandalous ways on an illness.

Vera was beyond the level of repair, and there was nothing or no one who could save her, and Daddy knew that. He spent most of his life trying to play captain save a hoe with Vera.

Low Down & Dirty Lovers

Daddy kneeled down beside her and coldly stared into her harsh eyes. The look the two of them shared spoke volumes that only they could understand. I saw the hurt and pain in his eyes, but I had no clue what else his stare held. He y snatched the wedding band that Vera wore on her ring finger. She didn't deserve it, she'd broken their vows many years ago. She was so scandalous she wore her wedding ring every time she did her dirty deeds.

Daddy looked at me, grabbed me by the chin, and stared into my big brown eyes.

"Chasity, I love you with all my heart. Please bear with me until I get myself together and send for you. NO matter what the situation is or where I'm at, you'll always be my one and ONLY princess," he said as he rubbed my chin with his thumb. "Joe, get your bitch ass out here." He yelled for JoeLee.

I stood on my tiptoes and whispered in my daddy's ear. "What about Wonderland? How would I ever go there if you are not here?"

He turned and faced me as if he wanted to cry. "This isn't forever," he said.

When JoeLee appeared, he hugged both of us tightly and planted kisses on our cheeks. "I love you two with all my heart. I'm not leaving because of you two. I just can't stand the sight of yawl's no good of a whore mother another day."

We both shook our heads, letting Daddy know we understood. Truth be told, I didn't understand at all why he was leaving us behind in such a shitty situation. Why couldn't he take us with him? Why couldn't we struggle together as a family? At that moment, I loved my father with all my heart but I resented him for his foul decision.

He gazed at Vera, who was still lying on the floor, then kneeled down beside her again and hawked spit in her face. "Vera, I'm done with you. I have a new woman who loves me and respects me."

Those were Daddy's last words as he walked out of our lives forever. A part of me knew he was never coming back.

From that day on, I grew even more hatred and resentment toward Vera. I couldn't stand the sight or thought of her. She didn't deserve to take another breath. I wanted her *dead*... She was my worst enemy, my worst nightmare and the cause of the bitterness I held within me. She was my hell on earth.

Chapter 1

It's Been Too Long

This had to be the hottest summer ever in my sixteen years of living. I sat on my front stoop and stared onto Atlantic Ave. The streets were crowded, and it was very noisy outside with tourists and vacationers visiting Atlantic City.

I fanned myself with the folded up newspaper, dying to catch a breeze.

"I'm going to kick your ass!" I said aloud as I pushed the foot of my growing fetus.

I had been carrying this baby for eight and a half months too long, and I felt nothing but pure hatred for this kid. The way it made me crave food, the way it took over my body and made me feel like I was the prisoner, the way it kicked me all throughout the day, and the damn night. This baby made my ass itch!

I made a promise to myself that this was the last child I was going to ever birth. No more doing favors for anyone else. After this, I was going to be all for   myself and myself only.

"Chasity," Vera yelled. "He's waiting for you. Get your ass in here now!"

I rolled my eyes as I got up, held my back for a little support, and wobbled my way into the house.

I stood before Vera with my hands on my hips as my belly poked out and rolled my eyes at her. She was sky high and didn't have a care in the world. I swear I hated this woman so much that every sight of her made me want to wring her fucking neck.

"Where is he at and what do he want?" I asked with much attitude.

"He's in my room," Vera replied in a slurred voice. "He wants some of that pregnant puss and some of that good ole milk."

I went into the kitchen and retrieved a plastic Ziploc bag for the breast milk. This sick son of a gun was going to have to take the breast milk to go. My nipples were rock hard and sore. No one was touching them today, and I didn't care what anyone said.

I walked into Vera's room where the fat son of a gun was lying across the bed butt naked. His penis was already standing north and wrapped in a condom. He took one look at me, not caring that I looked like a boy and dressed like a boy. All he cared about was the pregnant puss that he was going to get. Besides, after I dropped my clothing, with a pregnant belly and all, I still had the body of a goddess. I rolled my eyes and sucked my teeth as I removed my clothing and got on top of him.

The only sounds in the room were his heavy breathing and the condom rubbing against my dry insides. I sped my pace up, trying to get over this nightmare as fast as possible; the bed began to creak with each thrust. I tried to allow my mind to wander off to Wonderland, but there was no way in hell I could take this fat bastard to *MY* place.

I looked down at the sick man and he had a humongous silly smile on his face. I wanted to grab the feathered pillow and smother the life out of him, then get a butcher knife from the kitchen and stab Vera to death.

My mind was always on death as I lived each miserable day through this horrid storm.

Ever since Daddy left, Vera had been selling JoeLee and my souls to the devil, not to mention her own soul.

I couldn't take living life zoned out like a zombie anymore. JoeLee will turn eighteen in four months, and he planned to flee the home. I planned to leave as soon as I gave birth to my second child.

Our family was very sick and dysfunctional. Every day, I imagined Daddy sending for us like he promised. I had to get over it, he wasn't coming back. It had been too long since he'd made and broken that promise. I knew if I didn't do something quick I was going to be stuck in this situation forever.

"I'm done," the sick man roared. "Now get the hell off of me. You dazing off took all the fun out of it. Let me suck on your breast and get my milk so I can go."

I was so out of it that I hadn't realized the man had cum many seconds ago. The only thing that occupied my mind was why me? What did I do to deserve this cruel punishment?

I slid off him and grabbed my right breast with one hand and the zip lock bag with the other. With one squeeze, my breast milk began to flow.

I squeezed as much milk as possible into the bag while the fat fucker huffed and puffed as if he was getting annoyed.

I closed the bag shut, threw it at him, and started putting my clothes back on.

"No, I want to suck on your breast," he said with attitude. "I paid Vera to do so."

He grabbed me, pushed me onto the bed, grabbed one of my swollen sore nipples, and stuffed it into his oversized mouth.

I closed my eyes as he stole the candy, which was my milk from my baby.

It was all over a few minutes later. He walked out with a satisfied smile on his face and a pocket full of breast milk. When I got up and went into the bathroom to wash up, I caught JoeLee leaned over on the toilet getting fucked in the ass by one of his many clients. This particular client JoeLee was in love with. He swore this man was going to leave his wife for him.

"Ugh, I'm so tired of all these sick people," I cried as I rushed to my room and slammed the door.

After Daddy left, JoeLee and I were forced to be sex slaves. I hated it, while JoeLee enjoyed every second of it, just like Vera. Those two white liver fucks made me sick! Vera didn't have to ask or force JoeLee into doing anything; he was already down with the get down. JoeLee and I were like night and day, the complete opposite.

Our home was a wreck and it was embarrassing. Everyone in the neighborhood knew exactly what went on in our home. I was tired of the shameful stares and the bad mouthing I got every time I stepped foot outside. People talked and looked, but no one dared help us. When people spoke about our house, it was always mentioned as the sick family, or the house full of prostitutes, trannys and bull dikes.

Vera didn't give a rat's ass about me and JoeLee. I knew for sure she hated me, and maybe she cared about JoeLee a little bit, because he was willing to do whatever it took to please her. For that reason, I know she favored him more.

She didn't clothe us nor feed us.

One day I walked into her bedroom and cried to her that I was hungry.

Low Down & Dirty Lovers

My stomach was on 'E.' I hadn't eaten for two whole days. My stomach turned as I watched Vera sit on the edge of her bed butt naked with her legs wide open. The stinky aroma of hot sex glided through the air and filled my nostrils, which had me swallowing my own vomit. Vera was digging in her puss with two of her fingers as if she was digging for gold.

"What! I'm trying to get this damn condom out of me," she snapped. "That little dick bastard wore a condom three times too big for him, now it's stuck up in me. Are you going to give me a damn hand or just stand there and watch?"

I rolled my eyes. Vera was really a sick person that needed help. There was no way in hell I was going to stick my hands in her old stretched out vagina. If I was in hell and given an ultimatum to stick my fingers inside her and dig out the condom for a cold glass of water, or to continue to swallow my own hot spit, I would turn down the cold glass of water, and swallow my own spit with no questions asked!

"No, I'm not helping you! That's nasty. When are you going to buy some food?" I asked. "JoeLee and I are hungry." I figured that if I threw JoeLee's name in there, she would give us some money to get some food.

"Then you better get it how you live," she said as she stuffed her whole hand up in her vagina. She scrunched her face up like the pain was unbearable. Yeah right! That loose vagina of hers could take two fists up it. "I done did my part, yawl are old enough to fend for yawl selves. GET IT HOW YOU LIVE!"

I walked out of the room and slammed the bedroom door. How was she going to tell us to get it how we live? I thought her making us fuck men for money was getting it how we live, or in my case, getting it how she wanted us to live.

JoeLee and I did what we had to do to put food in our mouths and clothes on our back. Twice a week, we would walk up in down, Atlantic or Pacific Ave., or wherever we would see a stray hooker and rob her for her money. Before picking our victims, we would watch them for hours as they got in and out of cars, or went into dark alleys and served tricks five minutes of fantasies. Most of the time we would catch the hooker before they went in or broke their pimp off.

The money we got was good until pimps and prostitutes started to play the game with a little bit more caution. They would take the hoe's money after every trick, or the stray hoes would have someone out there who drove to hand their money over to. We had to start stealing money from Vera, or JoeLee would have sex with a trick and get extra money to feed the two of us. Which he only did for a week or two before he got tired of feeding me.

I would find all types of little side hustles to put food in my mouth. Fuck the clothing, I wore what I had or would go without.

Hungry, I walked outside and sat on my front porch. I stared at the cars as they passed me by, then I saw a hopeless cat limping across the street. It appeared that a car may have hit it. Narrowing my eyes, I crept behind the cat as it limped its way into an empty alley. The cat's pitiful cries told of its pain.

I picked up a brick and walked closer to the cat. "Here, kitty kitty," I called out in a sick and twisted voice.

The cat turned around and came closer to me. He never once took his eyes off me. He just knew I was his savior. I lifted the brick up to my chest and bashed the cat right in the face. With so much force, I bashed it in the face again. Blood and brain matter splattered all over my shirt. I couldn't believe what had come over me. Hurt people hurt people, and innocent bystanders. I was beyond hurt, but I couldn't believe I took my pain out on that innocent cat. I turned around to see if anyone was looking. Noticing no one was around to witness my brutality, I ran off to the house where I hopped in the shower, trying to wash the pain away from me. No matter how hard I scrubbed, I was still that same old wounded little girl …

I lay on my princess bed looking up at the ceiling and began to weep. I was really losing my mind; I knew I couldn't last one more second in this home. My life here was really fucked up. I had a confused tranny for a brother, a pushover who left me for a father, and a white liver prostitute who pimped her own children for a mother. I was very confused; I dressed like a boy, wore my hair like a boy, and walked and talked like a boy. My confusion reached its peak when the hell between my thighs started to rise and I thought about the only man I ever loved and ever wanted to love, *my father*.

"I hate it here, I hate myself, and I hate my life." I said aloud and began to cry.

My unborn child wasn't for me crying today. It started to go wild and kick my insides.

"You bastard, stop kicking me!" I yelled as if it was sitting next to me.

I couldn't take any more of this bastard kicking me.

I began to punch myself in the stomach repeatedly, hitting the little bastard back.

Although it hurt badly, I wasn't for the bullshit today. I was going to fight this bastard with any means.

As the pain shot up my body, I bit down on my bottom lip and continued to beat my stomach. I won the fight as the kicking finally stopped.

With my eyes closed, I lay there, wishing for a better life. I reached under my pillow and grabbed my safe haven. I stared at the ceiling as I took the blade and lightly ran it across my wrist. Finding the right spot, I pressed down harder as I felt my flesh peacefully splitting in half. I sighed and took a good breath. The self-inflicted would felt so damn good. I wasn't trying to take myself to a place where I could never come back; I just needed a temporary fix. Some chose drugs. That was their choice like this was my choice. I bit down on my bottom lip, taking the blade deeper and deeper into my flesh until I couldn't take any more.

Blood trickled down my arm and onto the sheets. I slid the blade back under the pillow, now with a look of rejoicing on my face. I was no cutter. I didn't do it too often; I just loved a temporary fix of painn.

As soon as I heard the bathroom door open, I got up and made my way to the bathroom.

"Ahhh!" I grunted and fell to my knees and squeezed my legs tightly as a sharp pain shot up my back.

"JoeLee!" I screamed out for help.

I knew this feeling well, too damn well to be my age. I was in labor.

JoeLee and Vera came to my aid and helped me off the floor. As soon as I stood up, blood mixed with other fluids ran down my legs.

By the time we made it to the hospital, I had already dilated four centimeters.

Two hours later, I gave birth to my second child.

"Here is your baby girl," the nurse said and tried to hand me the baby.

"Get that bastard out of my face," I spoke through gritted teeth as I brushed the child away from me. I knew to detach myself from this child. I couldn't love her, she wasn't mine to begin with. Vera had already sold her, so my heart knew better. No matter how much I wanted to loved her, I just couldn't.

The nurse and doctors were surprised at my actions but did as told. At that moment, all I wanted was my best friend, my blade that did magical justification to my life. Instead, I was granted medication where I could get some rest and temporarily forget about the unbearable hell that rested between my thighs.

A few hours later, I woke up to a cold pitcher of water being tossed on me.

My eyes flung open and I stared directly into Vera's cold eyes. "We have company," she said.

I turned and noticed our company then rolled my eyes and huffed with a nasty attitude.

Vera and the Clarks were in the room with me. Mrs. Clark was holding the baby, rocking her back and forth as the baby cooed. She played like she was a proud mother; she acted like she had just birthed the baby herself.

"She looks just like you," she said to Mr. Clark.

I kept my eyes closed and tried to ignore them. These people were beyond sick. I didn't want anything to do with those sickos.

Vera had met Mr. Clark three and a half years ago. He was one of her tricks and always had her doing wild things. Like sexing her on the hood of his car, just as the sun went down. I guess he got some kind of kick out of public sex. On top of that, he had his other sick fantasies like her urinating on him and giving him brown showers. Vera tried to introduce him to me, to dig deep down in his pockets, but he didn't like the idea of sexing little girls, so he always passed.

One day he came to Vera with a proposition that she just couldn't resist. He and his wife had been trying to conceive for many years, with no luck at all. So he made a promise to his wife that he was going to give her a baby before she left this earth. He offered Vera $10,000 to get her pregnant. Vera couldn't have any more children, her tubes were tied and burnt after she had given birth to me. There was no way in hell that Vera was going to let that much money walk right past her like that. So she offered my unwilling services to Mr. Clark. At first he turned her down, but knowing that this was once in a lifetime chance he changed his mind.

After having a talk with Mrs. Clark, she was down for it. The child could pass for hers and Mr. Clark's child, being that Mr. Clark was a half-breed. A white woman walking around with a complete Negro baby would have raised a red flag. Being the prominent attorney she was, she didn't want any questions asked about the ethnicity of her child.

Almost nine months later, I gave birth to my first child, which was a boy. I can't even tell you what he looked like; I gave him away without taking one look at him. That son of a gun was so damn loud. To this very day, his loud screams continue to haunt me.

Mrs. and Mr. Clark weren't satisfied; they had a beautiful, healthy baby boy, yet they wanted a girl too. So Mr. Clark impregnated me once again. Luck was on my side when I gave birth to a baby girl. If it was a boy, they were going to take that baby too and try for a girl, and keep trying until we had a little girl.

I was thankful that I was blessed with a girl. I couldn't bear being pregnant once again, let alone having Mr. Clark sex me and fill my insides up with his baby making juices for hours and hours. He was very attractive, but his ugly ways made him look so damn horrible.

Two days later, the baby and I left the hospital. As soon as we stepped foot outside, the Clarks were waiting for us in their car.

"Why are you doing this to me?" I asked Vera, staring into her cold eyes.

She stared right back at me for a second as the sinister smile left her face. She was now wearing a solemn expression. "Chas, baby girl, you know it was wrong of you to sleep with that man and get pregnant. I told you over and over I wasn't about to raise anyone's babies. I'm too young to be a grandmomma and you are sure as hell too young to be a momma. You did what was best for that child," she said in a serious tone.

Low Down & Dirty Lovers

I stared at her as if she was crazy. If looks could kill, she would be long DEAD! I couldn't believe this devil dressed in a cheap ass pink dress wearing red lipstick. How dare she try to pull this shit on me? I didn't sleep with anyone intentionally. All this was forced, none by choice, NEVER! Her reverse physiology wasn't going to drive me up the wall any longer.

"Are you serious, Vera? Are you fucking serious?" I asked.

She slid her sunglasses on her face. "I don't know what they drugged you up on in there," she said and walked to the car.

A part of me wanted to run off with my child, but I couldn't. How could I raise a child when I could barely fend for myself?

Immediately, I handed over the baby, as Vera took the cash from Mr. Clark. She licked her lips as she counted out $10,000.

"Thank you for blessing us with another beautiful child," Mrs. Clark said as she planted kisses all over the baby. I couldn't believe that she attended church every Sunday as if she was all holy. That woman was a hypocrite, a damn devil in disguise.

I didn't say a word as I sat in the back seat looking out the window. I was lost in my own thoughts, thinking that this couldn't be life. And the main question that I always pondered on … Why me?

Vera sat on the opposite side of me, counting her money over and over with a grin on her face.

"She should be back and ready within a month or two, and we can work on yawl's child," Vera said.

She was a damn lie! There was no more baby making for me. I wish JoeLee's faggot ass was able to birth a baby. I knew JoeLee would love sweating in pain and pushing a baby out. Matter of fact, if anyone else wanted any more kids, they better find a way to push one out of JoeLee's dick or Vera's old played out ass better birth one.

I was furious and sick to my stomach. I looked over at Vera, who was still counting the money for the ninetieth time. In the front, Mr. Clark drove, while Mrs. Clark sat turned around in her seat playing with the baby, who sat in her car seat. Her purse sat in the middle.

We stopped at a red light and my mind was already made up. I should have done this a long time ago when my daddy left. I had to get away from this situation before I ended up hurting someone or myself. I felt dead; I knew it was a life out there somewhere, my life at that.

I reached over, snatched the money out of Vera's hands, grabbed Mrs. Clark's purse, and fled the scene.

"Chasi-----ty!" I heard Vera yell out as I ran like a thief in the night.

In the process, I knocked over a prostitute who was working the day shift on the blade. Without any apologies, I kept running.

As I turned the corner, I felt my fresh stitches tear, which I couldn't have cared less about. Four blocks later, I slowed down and checked to make sure no one was behind me. No one was there, so I searched Mrs. Clark's purse and grabbed all the money out of it, along with the credit cards and her ID, and ditched the purse.

I straightened up my baggy sweat pants, fixed my wife beater and wiped the sweat from my forehead as I bopped down the street with a pocket full of money, along with a few credit cards. Still not knowing what my next move was going to be, but I knew I had to think of something quick. The last thing I wanted to do was be on the streets by nightfall.

The only safe place I knew was my girlfriend Kim's house. Neither Vera nor JoeLee knew where she lived.

Kim was someone I had met a year ago. I confided in her as a friend, and one thing led to another and we became lovers. She was always there when I needed her, or a shoulder to lean on. She was the first female to turn me out. When she went down on me, it felt like a walk into heaven. I returned the gesture and had her pulling my hair and screaming for hours. After my first taste, I was in love with the cat and I became a complete carpet muncher.

I knocked on Kim's door and she opened up dressed in nothing but a sheer nightgown. I licked my lips at the sight of her hardened nipples and her apple bottom as both protruded from underneath the sheer. She welcomed me in.

"What's the matter, pumpkin pie?" Kim asked as she read the expression on my face.

Only Kim knew most of my problems, and she was the only person who had open ears when I needed to talk.

"I just gave birth to my second and last child, or should I say, their child," I huffed as I sat down on the old torn up leather sofa in Kim's living room.

"Damn, pumpkin." Kim sat next to me and rubbed her hand up and down my back. "I'm so sorry that you have to go through all of this bullshit. I wish there were something I could do. You know what, Chasity? You are never going back there again. You can stay here with me and my momma until we come up with further plans."

I kissed her soft lips, thanking her as she spoke the words that I wanted to hear. I needed someone to help me break free from the world that I was in. I knew she would come through right when I needed her.

One kiss led to a sweet ole sweaty sex session in her bedroom. I performed all of the new tricks she'd taught me a few weeks ago, which had her screaming in ecstasy. When we were finished, she lay in my arms and we drifted off to a catnap.

When we woke up, I showed Kim the credit cards and kept the cash a secret. I learned to never let the right hand know what the left hand was doing years   ago.

"Yo, son! That whore got a black card," Kim said in excitement. She just knew she was about to shop her ass off.

I pulled out Mrs. Clark's ID and showed it to Kim. She took once glance at it and handed it back to me.

"I think we got us a Mrs. Clark. My momma will play that part today," she said as she picked up the phone and called her momma.

Theresa, Kim's momma, was there within a matter of minutes. Kim placed the ID next to her face and she sure enough was a perfect match to use the ID.

Before leaving out, I plugged my cell phone up to the charger. Vera wasn't giving up, I had over thirty missed calls and fifteen text messages. Calls were from Vera and her butt buddy, JoeLee. I turned my phone back off and placed the two people who were once family in the back of my mind.

I pondered if I should go back for JoeLee, but I dismissed that ridiculous thought. JoeLee was my brother, but he didn't give a damn about me. Besides, his problems at home were something he could handle, and he enjoyed it very much.

Thinking about his punk ass made me sick to my stomach. I remember when Daddy first left and it finally hit Vera like a truckload of bricks, she started to act out even worse.

I woke up one morning to find her and JoeLee standing over me. The sun beamed into my bedroom, nearly blinding me as I wiped the morning crust out of my eyes.

"Gon' ahead, Joe, fuck her," Vera said in a drunken slur.

I couldn't believe my ears as she said the most preposterous thing I had ever heard. I just knew my ears were deceiving me.

"Ewww, Vera. I'm not fucking her," JoeLee said as he turned his nose up. "That is just nasty." He gawked at me as if I had cooties or something.

I sighed with relief when I heard those words coming from my older brother. I knew him and I had somewhat of a bond. We were supposed to protect one another from harm, and never do harm to each other.

"Why not? It's natural. We are all God's children," Vera snapped. She hated the word 'NO,' especially when it was used toward her.

"Vera, she has a coochie. I don't want no cat. If she was my brother, I promise you, Vera, I would do her."

I couldn't believe what JoeLee punk ass said. If I were a boy, he would sex me? That shit was just bogus to me.

I jumped out of bed and pounced on JoeLee, knocking him to the floor. I landed powerful blows onto his face, fighting like a man.

JoeLee fought back with light smacks and a whole lot of scratches, trying to claw me up like a cat.

This was pure excitement for Vera as she watched her only two kids go at it like strangers, trying to knock each other's head off. She cheered us on until we finally got tired of fighting each other and stopped.

That wasn't it for Vera, she demanded that we fight and not stop until we knocked each other out. She wanted to see bloodshed and all.

I wasn't going to fight my flesh and blood like that, and I thought that JoeLee wouldn't either. He proved me wrong and found the man that was hiding within him and started to fight me like a man. I didn't give up and did everything in my power to protect myself. My bedroom had turned into a boxing ring and JoeLee and I were the contenders. JoeLee was the heavyweight boxer and I was the lightweight who was not giving up. Of course, Vera was the announcer who cheered us on.

Within minutes, I knocked JoeLee's bitch ass out. Had him sprawled across the floor, which satisfied Vera. From that day out, JoeLee and I bumped heads and always ended up having a boxing match to settle our beef.

My mind was made up. JoeLee was staying where he liked it most. There he could get all the dick in the ass he wanted. He was in dick heaven, why would I take him out of his heaven?

The outlets were around the corner from us, so we were there in a matter of minutes. Before shopping, we decided to go out to eat first. We visited one of the finest restaurants in town, Ruth's Chris Steakhouse. The steaks there were priced outrageously, but none of us gave a damn. It wasn't our money, compliments to Mrs. Clark for the delicious meal. Afterward, we hit up all of the top of the line stores. This shopping spree was not going to be cheap at all.

Coach, Chanel, Louis Vuitton you name it we were there. I allowed Kim and her momma to get whatever they wanted. This was free money and had no restrictions. I shopped at all the exclusive stores as well, buying all the clothing I ever dreamed to have. I used to say to myself that once I got some money, I was going to have Polos to last me a lifetime. From the Polo outlet, I literally bought the store out. Buying every color Polo they had in stock, with matching snap back hats and shoes.

At the cash registers, Kim's momma, who pretended to be Mrs. Clark, would whip out the card while flashing a big smile. Our mischievous acts were never questioned, as she was the perfect match for Mrs. Clark.

Before we made it back home, I purchased new furniture and bedroom sets for Kim and her momma's house, decking it out.

Later that night, Kim and I lay in *our* new bedroom, playing the happiest couple alive. Although it wasn't my money, what I had done for Kim, no other female or male had ever done for her before.

Low Down & Dirty Lovers

When Kim was sound asleep, I went into the bathroom and counted my money. It was a total of $13,000 in all. The $10,000 I took from Vera and the $3,000 I took from Mrs. Clark. I took out $3,000, wrapped the rest in a plastic bag and placed it inside the toilet tank. I knew my money was safe there. Kim and her momma weren't the cleanest females alive, so I knew the chances of them finding my money there were slim to none.

For a few weeks, Kim and I lived the fairytale relationship. We would sex all day and night, get high on the best weed. Have all types of drinks. Kim would cook for me while I spoiled and pampered her. Treating her like the Queen she wasn't made out to be.

Chapter 2

All Good Things Come to an End

One day, Kim and I decided to go shopping. We already had more than enough things, but we wanted more, or should I say she wanted more. She had a taste of the finer things in life and lost all control. Kim and I sat outside on the front as we waited for her momma to come home.

It had been a month since I stole Mrs. Clark's credit card, and two and a half weeks since I last used it. I don't know how much we spent on it, but I knew it was over the thousands. We were balling out of control and buying any and everything that the black card would allow us to purchase. We knew to stay away from big things such as cars. I badly wanted to buy Kim and me a car, but her momma said that was a big no-no. A car would only bring heat to us if Mrs. Clark *ever* reported her card stolen, and the last thing we needed was heat.

When I first moved in with Kim, I had the cash to purchase us a car, but over time, I had been dipping in my stash. Now there wasn't much left at all.

Low Down & Dirty Lovers

Kim had been getting on my last nerve. She was always complaining, but I managed to put up with her. Being with her had me questioning whether I wanted to deal with females. Just sexing one was fun, and women always made me cum versus a man. It was just something about a woman's touch that drove me wild. I just couldn't handle all the complaining and bickering.

We had just got back from the mall, trying to use the card, which had declined.

"Chas, you need to get up and get a job or something," Kim complained as she leaned on top of the kitchen island. "You are my man. You are supposed to be my provider."

I puffed on the good marijuana that I had been smoking on before I spoke. "Girl, what you talking about? Don't I provide for you enough? You got the flyest gear, good marijuana. Hair and nails done, and not to mention I been wining and dining your ass."

I couldn't believe Kim and her attitude. I practically made the bitch, and here she was complaining like I haven't done shit for her.

"I know, and I'm thankful for everything you have done … but now that we can't use the card, what are we going to do?" Kim whined.

I couldn't handle Kim and her nagging; this was all too much for me. She was about to blow a good high, and I wasn't going to let that happen.

I grabbed my New York Yankees snapback hat and my cell phone and left the house without telling Kim shit. She wanted me to provide for her, me being the person I was … I was going to get out and get it how I lived for my girl.

Just how JoeLee and I used to get it how we lived months ago, I was back at it again. This time providing for my greedy girl and me. I had to admit, I had it bad for Kim. Anything that girl wanted, at the snap of a finger I was there giving her my all. She asked and she got, and that's just how it was when it came to Kim. My heart was weak for her.

I walked up and down Atlantic Avenue until I found the three victims. The first two ended up breaking their pimp off before I got my hands on their purses. The other one was walking down the street looking lost.

When I got up closer to her, I noticed she had a face full of tears. Fuck feeling sorry for her, no one ever felt bad for me, no matter what I went through. Her purse was dangling off her right shoulder, I quickened my pace, and when I got near her, I snatched her purse and ran.

By the time she realized what happened, I had already taken off around the corner. I dumped the purse of the contents and took the little money she had, which was only $183. It was better than nothing at all.

One thing a beggar or a thief can't be is picky.

I walked to a strip club and paid the $20 admission to enter. All the best dancers were there shaking their asses tonight. I sat at the bar next to a guy who was dressed in a blue and white pin stripe suit. On his feet he wore a pair of shiny blue gator shoes that looked like they had been greased with cooking oil. His head was covered with a hat that had a feather sticking from the side of it. He drank out of an oversized pimp cup. Knowing how pimps got down, he was surely sipping on nothing but the finest.

I tapped my right foot on the stool as I took another glance at him. Both of his pinky fingers were covered in humongous diamond pinky rings. The rings were so big it was ridiculous; no doubt they were weighing his pinky fingers down. On his neck, he wore a big gold rope chain. He flashed a quick smile at me, showing off his two fangs that were gold with diamonds in the middle.

Low Down & Dirty Lovers

While the bartender took her time to approach me for my drinks, I sat and wondered if the diamonds in his mouth were real or not.

"Yeah, bitch," the pimp answered his phone. "Bitch, I don't care how hot it is out there. You better duck and dodge them blue and white boys and get my fucking money, hoe."

My insides tickled as I sat and listened to him curse out his hoe. I knew if she didn't get his money, she was going to be a beat down hoe tonight.

I ordered a double shot of Patron on the rocks and rocked side to side in my chair as I impatiently waited for my drink. Looking out the corner of my eye, I could see the pimp gawking at my moneymakers and my double D's.

He was no fool. Even with all the baggy clothing I wore, he was still able to get a good glimpse at my goddess possessions. I rolled my eyes at him and sucked my teeth. Letting him know, to stop looking.

"You got some big ole titties," he said in a thick southern accent. "I see the woman you trying to hide." He cracked a smile.

I turned my head as if I didn't hear a word he said. He was disrespectful, and I wasn't about to entertain the fool. He finally got the hint.

For the next hour or so, I threw shots back and listened to the pimp throw game down on every chick that passed him, trying to hire him a new worker. His pimp game was vicious. By the end of the night, he succeeded and walked out with two of the baddest strippers in the club. One on his left arm and the other on the right.

"Daddy gon' take good care of you, as long as you two take good care of me." His voice echoed as he exited the club. At that moment, I was infatuated with the power of his words and the game he spat at the women.

I left the club furred; I was so drunk I wasn't able to walk without falling to the ground. Still, I managed to make my way home.

When I got there, all the lights were off. Apparently, Kim was so mad that I left her with an attitude that she didn't bother to open the door. It was no sweat off my back; I didn't feel like putting up with her nasty attitude anyways. Her cracking slick would've only caused my drunk behind to knock her teeth down her throat tonight.

I sat on the front stoop and watched the nightlife in Atlantic City. It was crazy how so many strange things went on. Nearly every female out there tonight was doing something strange for a little change. Including Vera! I watched her walk up in down the blade, being the oldest hoe on the strip. Trying to strut what she didn't have. If I weren't so drunk, I would rob her for every red cent she had on her.

A car pulled up alongside her and I watched as she bent over, flirting with the trick, trying to get him to spend money on her.

Out of nowhere, a pimp ran up behind her, grabbed her by her ponytail, and pulled her away from the car.

The driver was frightened and pulled off, not wanting any parts of what was about to go down.

Instead of beating Vera for working the blade without a pimp, he made her empty her purse and took every penny she had on her.

Watching her get robbed had tears in my eyes from laughing so hard. I hadn't had this much excitement since Daddy beat the shit out of her and left. The look on her face was priceless as she stormed off.

I woke up the next morning to the sun beaming down on me, letting me know it was time to get my ass up. The sun had to have just made its entrance for the day because I could still hear the birds chirping.

Low Down & Dirty Lovers

As soon as I got up, the terrible hangover from last night's drinking began to kick my ass. My head started to spin. Before I could make it off the front porch, I vomited everywhere.

Oh well, Kim was going to have to get that shit up later!

I was about to knock on the door, but it flung open. A strange man stepped out and brushed past me.

"What's up, homie?" he saide.

I returned the greeting by nodding my head back at him.

Kim was standing in the screen door wearing her favorite pink robe. I could tell by how she was holding it close that she was completely naked underneath.

I was no fool; my girl, who I thought was a lesbian, couldn't help but have the stick too. That's why she never opened the door for me, leaving me to sleep outside on the porch. I'm outside while she's inside fucking in a house that I had been paying the bills for.

"What's up, Kim?" I asked.

"Chas, come on, don't act like you didn't know. Sometimes I need a little poking and leaving all the joking alone. This lesbo shit is a joke, and I want no parts of it no more. Besides, you are too young for me."

Her words were hurtful and they stung me like a bee. I had to man up. I knew how whores like Kim were. When your money ran out or got low, they were on to the next. I held my head up high. "So what are you saying?" I asked like I didn't already know.

"I'm just saying, Chas, we can always be friends, but you can no longer live here." She ranted in a tone that I didn't appreciate.

"Oh, it's cool. Let me get my shit and I will be on my way. I should have seen this coming. When I had money, you were all on my dick. When I go broke you leave me high and dry?"

Kim opened the door and allowed me to get my belongings, which I packed in one book bag. I went into the bathroom, lifted the toilet lid, and retrieved the rest of the cash I had left over, which was no more than $500.

My head hung low as I walked to the front door. I was yet again miserable.

"Sorry." Kim shook her head as I approached the door.

"Yeah, me too," I dryly replied.

WHAM! I punched Kim in her face, which sent her flying to the floor. She whimpered like the bitch she was. "Bitch, I'm sorry that I ever met you!"

I don't know why she thought I was going to leave that easy. Now that I was satisfied, I jumped off the porch with my book bag on my back and started down the street.

"Chasity, you knocked my fucking tooth out!" Kim yelled as she chased after me.

I turned around and stared at her bloody face. It was apparent that I had knocked her tooth out, but I didn't give a damn. Shit like that happens when you use someone for what they have. What the hell? She thought it wasn't going to be no repercussions, or did she think I was a punk or something? Either way she got what was coming to her.

I held my fist up in the air, letting her know that I would kindly knock another tooth out if she wanted to fuck with me.

She got the point and decided to back down and take her toothless ass back in the house before she lost another tooth.

I bopped to the nearest bodega. My stomach was talking to me and I needed to put something in it.

"Pops, let me get a ham and cheese sandwich."

Low Down & Dirty Lovers

I grabbed a bag of Bar B Q chips to munch on and a Pepsi soda.

It only took a few minutes for my sandwich to be made. Afterward, I paid for my items and bopped back out the store.

Five hundred dollars to my name and no place to go, it sucked. It always sucked for me. I walked a few blocks over to Pacific Ave and went to the barbershop to cop me some weed. I needed something to clear my mind.

Afterward, I sat on someone's stoop and ate my sandwich and chips, then washed downed my snack down with my Pepsi.

I couldn't believe that bitch had the nerve to put me out. I badly wanted to go back to her house and knock the rest of her teeth down her throat, hoping she would choke and die off her own teeth. I couldn't go back there, or go back home. No way in hell would I go back home and deal with that shit Vera had put me through. This pussy was mine, and it wasn't for sale and never would be! Over my dead body!

Bopping back down the block, I ran into someone who could purchase me a room. $130 paid for the whole week.

Peering over the balcony of the roach infested hotel, I watched as the hookers worked the blade. It wasn't shit else to do. I couldn't take watching them whores any longer. I was broke and homeless and needed to make moves quick.

I glanced over at the Trump Plaza Casino sign that was calling my name. Something was telling me to go in there and try my luck. I bopped through the lobby of the casino as if I owned the spot. My eyes lit up as I sat down at the slot machine. I hoped that today would be my lucky day, only if I hit the jackpot. I placed twenty dollars on the machine and ordered a drink.

Playing back and forth, my money went up and then back down. A few drinks later, I was nice and tipsy, and few hours later, I was nice and broke. Phony ass casino took all of my damn money, leaving me without a penny to my name. I was fucking hopeless. I should have quit while I was ahead.

What do niggas do when they are broke? Drink, of course! The drinks kept coming, and of course, I kept drinking. That was the only thing to do.

Going into the casino was simply a stupid mistake, just like fucking with Kim. I wanted to snap the hell out. Between Kim and these fucking slot machines, both had me in a fucked up position.

I walked out the casino, drunker than a skunk. The only thing I was able to do was go back to my room and sleep it off. I slept over the next two days, then decided to sleep the rest of the week. Hell, I was broke. What the hell could you do without money?

A knock on the door awakened me from my slumber. It was those fucking Arabs putting me out. I glanced over at the clock. It was only 11:35 AM and check out time wasn't until noon. Ignoring the rude knocks, I took my ass back to sleep and woke up at exactly 12:30. I placed my book bag on my back and walked down the street with no place to go.

For the next three days, I slept on the beach. Surprisingly, I slept peacefully. Nice and quiet, the only noise I heard was the noise from the filthy beach water that was speaking its own language.

The fourth night it began to storm.

This was my storm, Chasity's storms.

I looked up into the sky, which was black and purple. Lightning struck and thunder roared like a pack of lions. Call me weird, but the storm was talking to me. It was soothing, and I understood it as we together conversed in our own language. It was magical.

I grabbed my things and ran to the bar, my favorite bar. Too bad tonight I didn't have no money to drink or tip the strippers.

I sat at the end of the bar, lost in my own thoughts.

The bartender walked over to me and placed a drink in front of me.

"Sorry, love, I don't have no money tonight," I told her.

"It's cool, boo, it's on me." She flirted.

"What is it?"

"Jose Cuervo."

"Cool."

I threw the double shot back. After that first night out, Jose Cuervo had become one of my favorite drinks.

Over the next few hours, she continued to freely serve me Jose Cuervo. Each time, she made it a point to flirt with me. She was fine as all hell, so I didn't mind the flirting. I even flirted back a little. I just wish I had a place to take her, so I could get a taste.

It was crazy, I was always thinking like a nigga. Ole girl giving me drinks and here I am, wanting to smash her. Just like a nigga.

A pimp came and sat next to me. I peered down at his fancy shoes and his jewelry. It was the same pimp who had sat next to me at this very bar weeks ago.

"What's happening, youngin'?" he asked.

"Chilling, thinking of a master plan," I replied.

"A master plan, huh?"

"Sonny." He extended his manicured hand. Every one of his fingers was covered in diamond rings. Again, his pinky finger was graced with the biggest rings I'd ever laid eyes on.

"I'm Chas."

"Chas, pleased to meet you, pimping."

I shook his hand and cracked a small smile.

"Man, these hoes out here tripping. Always wanna be down with a pimp, but don't wanna get down for a pimp. You feel me?"

"Uh huh." I shook my head, not knowing what the hell he was talking about.

"This pimp shit is stressful, a pimp ready to retire. You feel me?"

I shook my head again. I didn't know that pimps could retire. Especially at such a young age. The way he was talking, I began to look at pimping with a whole new view. I now saw pimping as a job.

After a few hours of listening to him rant on, I basically knew the game, or at least the basics.

Thanks to Sunny, I was now an aspiring pimp.

The game was supposed to be sold not told, but since it was told to me for free, I decided to take that shit and run with it.

Sunny got up, left a $50 tip, and smoothly walked out the door. Just like a pimp in training, I got up and followed behind him.

That night I walked the block, watched the hookers, and learned some of the game on my own. The way Sonny was explaining the shit, it sounded a bit stressful. But he made it seem like a piece of cake. Always believing none of what I hear and half of what I see, I had to check things out for myself. I had nowhere to go, and nothing but time on my hands anyways.

Low Down & Dirty Lovers

Around 3:00 AM, things started to get a little slow. I watched as the pimps drove around and collected their money and their hoes to take it in for the night. Sitting back, I pondered if I should jump into something that I knew nothing about and really wanted no parts of, or should I just stick to what I knew? Robbing and thieving.

You better get it how you live! Vera's words popped into my head. That bitch was right. I better get it how I live. That was the only useful advice the worthless whore had given me.

"Daddy, it's slow out here and I only got $250 to my name?" I heard a girl say as she talked on the phone. It was apparent that it was her pimp.

"Why do I have to stay out here? I'm telling you, I won't be able to make another $500, not tonight," she whined.

Her beauty instantly caught my eyes. She was fine, and I wouldn't have thought as fine as she was, that she would be out on the blade selling her ass! As they say, never judge a book by its cover. It was the prettiest of them who were out doing the dirty work and acting as if they had something to prove.

I straightened my jeans up and ran my hands through my cornrows. Although I'd had this outfit on for the last three days, I knew I was still fresh to death. My Prada shoes still looked fresh, my Seven jeans were nice and clean. My braids were fresh. Truth to be told, I know I was looking right.

She walked back past me and I winked at her. She instantly held her head down and she looked at the ground.

"Daddy, I'm sorry. I will stay out here and make your money."

Just like Sonny said, an obedient hoe was the best hoe. Respect took you a long way.

"Psss." I hissed

153

She glanced over at me.

"If that nigga ain't treating you right, then move on," I said as I licked my lips. I'd always had a habit of licking my lips, and boy did the women love it too! That's how I always reeled them in, with my sexy, plush lips.

She didn't say anything, she just looked at me like I was a ghost or something.

I had a gift of gab, and tonight was the perfect time to use it. "Break bread with the right one. Be in it to win it. Don't make this a long-term goal, let's get this money and get out and retire early. Big whips, nice homes and expensive things, you dig, baby girl?" I said, stealing the words I heard Sonny use over the phone.

The girl was young, naïve, dumb and full of cum, and just needed direction. It was going to be my first time guiding someone, but I had faith in myself. I knew I could do it. Hell, if the rest of them clowns could pimp a bitch, I knew I could.

"So you wanna be my new daddy?" she asked.

"No doubt, bitch, is you trying to be down or what?"

"Oh, shit!" She jumped and ran behind me for cover.

A black ugly motherfucker passed by me in a beat up 1970 Cadillac.

She waited for him to pass by before she came from behind me. "That's my pimp."

"Nah, bitch, that was your ex-pimp. You looking at your new pimp now."

She needed a little push to move on from her old pimp, so push is exactly what I did. "Bitch, I know you don't have to think about shit. You fucking with that nigga with that Cadillac that's older than your damn grandmomma. Out with the old and in with the new. You better get with the program. Where all yawl money going to? You know that nigga is out tricking that shit off, as you out here busting your ass to make it. You better stop being a fool and get with Chas Money."

Chas Money, I liked that. I told y'all I had a gift of gab. That hoe was ready to move on.

"Chas Money, I like that. Okay, daddy, I'm down."

Just like that, I had a new bitch.

"Bitch then break bread." I held my hand out.

She went into her cheap Wal-Mart purse, pulled out her money, and handed it over to me, her new pimp.

I snatched the money and counted it. It totaled to $250, just like she told her ex-pimp.

My first hoe dollar had me feeling like a boss, that's what money does to you. In the end, it could make you, break you or take you…

http://www.amazon.com/Hell-Between-My-Thighs-Chasitys-ebook/dp/B013QCMW1S

Angel Williams & Lady Amethyst

Star City Publications Books

www.starcitypublications.com

Envy the Root of All Evil (Part 1)

Raven's Cravings

Momma I Ain't NO SAINT!

Gold Diggin' Honeys

Love On LockDown

Envy The Root Of All Evil (Part 2)

Pretty Money

Almighty Dolla (Anthology)

The Prodigal Son

Envy the Root Of All Evil (Part 3)

Promise Land

Ryder

Untamed And Deranged Mates

The Bentleys

Envy The Root Of All Evil (Part 4)

The Streets Can Wait But My Love Wont

Fou: Til Death Do Us Part

Lyfe Matters (Coming Soon)

Sins Of A Pastor (Coming Soon)

The Bentleys 2 (Coming   Soon)

Low Down & Dirty Lovers

Hell Between My Thighs

Thugs & The Chicks Who Love Em (Coming Soon)

www.ingramcontent.com/pod-product-compliance
Lightning Source LLC
Chambersburg PA
CBHW050324200626
46810CB00022B/1569